A Corner of the Veil

of the Veil

❧

Laurence Cossé

TRANSLATED FROM THE FRENCH BY
Linda Asher

FOREWORD BY
Jack Miles

SCRIBNER

SCRIBNER
1230 Avenue of the Americas
New York, NY 10020

SCRIBNER and design are trademarks of Jossey-Bass, Inc., used under
license by Simon & Schuster, the publisher of this work.

DESIGNED BY ERICH HOBBING

Set in Simoncini Garamond

Manufactured in the United States of America

1   3   5   7   9   10   8   6   4   2

Library of Congress Cataloging-in-Publication Data

Cossé, Laurence.
[Coin du voile. English]
A corner of the veil/Laurence Cossé; translated from the French
by Linda Asher; foreword by Jack Miles.
p.   cm.
I. Asher, Linda. II. Title.
PQ2663.07248C6713   1999
843'.914—dc21   98-50059
CIP

Originally published in French in 1996 as *Le Coin du Voile*
by Éditions Gallimard.

ISBN 0-684-84667-5

Foreword to Le Coin du Voile
by Laurence Cossé

"If nothing is serious," Oscar Wilde once wrote, "then nothing is funny." Laurence Cossé must take the God-question seriously, for she has written a hilarious God-novel. God appears in it only by way of a proof for His existence, whose unexpected discovery disrupts church and state alike, but just that much turns out to be enough.

Cossé has a wickedly keen eye for the foibles of both churchmen and statesmen. If she were a sculptor or a painter instead of a novelist, she would be Daumier, for with a caricaturist's economy, she does in a sentence what others cannot do in pages. Laughter is not the only pleasure she provides, however. The local color in this novel, mostly Parisian, is as agreeable and as effortlessly brought off as anything in Simenon and will charm American readers as much as that master of mystery ever did. As for suspense, *Le Coin du Voile* [A Corner of the Veil] has the elegance of a slender, perfect necklace—a thin chain from which hangs just a single, dazzling diamond. Try to take your eyes off it. You can't.

Cossé's "Casuists"—transparently, the French

Jesuits—are brought off with an attention to droll detail and an understated affection that recall the short stories of J. F. Powers about American Catholic priests in the 1950s. The distinct deshabille of a certain kind of no-longer-young cleric, still wearing old sweaters from his preordination years. The crotchety brilliance of a priestly intellectual who specializes, as one of her Casuists does, in *refuting* proofs for the existence of God. In these characterizations, Cossé makes the serious and the comic dance memorably together.

And finally, there is this writer's language. *Le Coin du Voile* was reviewed in Paris on the same day as the French translation of a book of mine entitled *God: A Biography*. I was amused by the review of Cossé, and my French publisher kindly bought me a copy of her book to read on my flight home. To speak simply, I was entranced. Perhaps because I have read too much French theory in recent years, I had come to think of late-twentieth-century French prose as terminally arch and vague. Cossé made me fall in love with the language again. Reading her, one remembers why *le mot juste* is a French phrase. She makes the language glow—as she makes the whole of this irresistible little book glow—with equal measures of clarity, intelligence, humor, and warmth.

JACK MILES
Los Angeles
January 15, 1999

PART ONE

The Casuists

Monday, 8:32 P.M.

Father Bertrand Beaulieu shut his office door behind him, considered the heaps of books, file folders, manuscripts, and newspapers in which other people would have seen ordinary disorder but whose meticulous order was clear to him, and concluded: yes, solitude was what he liked best. Every day, nearly every day, he asked himself the question: Was he happier in solitude, or in the company of his peers? Because his life required both that he be alone and that he never be alone. Evenings at seven-thirty, the dinner hour rang for him as a deliverance. He would work for five hours, six hours, in the afternoon (mornings he received visitors). Which did he enjoy more—settling down to write, finally? or finally quitting for the day? Evenings, he was eager to join his companions at dinner. And at that moment the answer was beyond doubt: it was they who were his pleasure. Their mere existence, the sound of their voices, of their coughs, their smells, their wit, their culture—the ever-fascinating shimmer of their collective knowledge—their crazes, their quirks . . .

But the meal over, his coffee cup still in hand, Beaulieu could not suppress it—he would be seized again with the desire to be off by himself. Inimitable coffee, pale and lukewarm, that existed only in "their houses," here in this land of utterly correct coffee; coffee that everyone joked about but no one managed to get changed; a mystery, a true mystery. Cup in a fake white porcelain glaze, inoffensive enough to look at, but distasteful to use. And every evening, at that same instant, the desire to be off by himself—no, the desire to *be* himself.

Yet Bertrand took only an hour off for dinner, seven-thirty to eight-thirty. After which, unless he had some lecture to give or discussion to lead, he would go back up to his office. That hour, though, was enough to change his mind. No question—for him, contentment lay in solitude.

Actually, he had no more patience for solitude than he had for the society of his peers, as was frequently remarked, with an eye on Bertrand and a hand on his own pipe stem, by his tablemate and confrère Father Thomas Blin (who was also a psychoanalyst and a late-night taxi driver).

At least, Bertrand thought as he went over to his office window, at least his own successive inclinations were themselves states of desire. Desire for people's presence, then desire for silence. He drew the curtains. The pulse of desire.

For instance, before dinner, the mere sight of the day's mail as yet unopened overwhelmed Bertrand: two inches thick, ten letters at least, which he would have to answer tonight because the next day would bring as many more. And then just an hour later—Why should that be? It was an hour of nothing special: a few words, a little smoke—the same pile of mail was somehow appealing. Sitting down, pencils to the right, felt tips to the left. In front of him, pads of paper. Order and silence, autonomy. The feel of a garden in the evening, well, yes. Checking his list of things-still-to-do, finding "mail," crossing out "mail."

One envelope larger than the others stuck out from the pile. It was also the only one made of cheap brown paper. Father Beaulieu pulled it out of the bundle. He had recognized the crazy writing that tilted its outsize characters over to the left, practically laying them flat. That lunatic was back again. A Martin Something who ten times already had sent Beaulieu—this same way, by mail—proof of the existence of God. Ten different demonstrations, one day by logic, three months later through chemistry, once by way of semantics, another time by way of the absurd, each time argued over fifteen or twenty pages, which Bertrand read through to the end each time. Because he answered. Well, he had answered in depth at least three of those mailings, anyway. The big envelope slid under the pile. He would do the others first.

*　　　*　　　*

At ten o'clock, Father Beaulieu was still at it. He who had the knack of answering so neatly in three lines—so very haiku—this evening had had to spend ten minutes on the simplest response. Nothing but heavy questions. Eleven "To the Editor." Not one "Bertrand, old friend," not one "Dear Uncle B."

The abortion article alone was responsible for three quarters of the letters. About as many letters of support as attacks. Support that brought Bertrand no pleasure—ideological, excessive: one might think they hadn't read the piece. Attacks that hurt. He should have ignored some lines. He'd certainly had to read them. "How does the Society of Casuists put up with a troublemaker like you in its midst?" . . . "They say job rotation is the rule with the Casuists, and that today's provincial works in the kitchen tomorrow. Sir, we ardently hope to hear that you have moved to the stoves. However execrable your cooking, it can never do the harm your writings do."

And offers to contribute to the magazine. Job inquiries. The table of contents for a thesis: the author proposed to publish it as is. A proposal—from a woman, nice, actually—to call the journal *Jesus* rather than *Outlooks*.

Ten twenty-five. Finally. Only the brown letter left to go. Beaulieu opened it, already exasperated. Dear God, the number of madmen You put into the world. The handwriting was dreadful, a kind of embroidery that left no margin right or left, top or bottom. There were only six sheets tonight, fewer than the other times. Beaulieu took a square of chocolate from the desk drawer and started reading.

Six pages farther, he was trembling. This time the proof was neither arithmetical, nor physical, nor esthetical, nor astronomical; it was irrefutable. The proof of God's existence had been achieved.

Bertrand was tempted, for a second, to toss the bundle into the wastebasket. The hour had come for the world's "great tribulation," as in Apocalypse VII:14. The powers of darkness were to launch their final battle against the manifest truth, and he was the voice, the tiny human voice, who must give the signal for the hostilities to begin.

But now he flung himself flat on his belly, his whole length, as on the day of his ordination.

How long did he stay on the floor? He sat up, looked at his watch: over an hour. He was suffocating, now, with something like joy. He had to talk to Hervé. Hervé was never asleep at midnight. Bertrand stood and picked up the telephone at the end of his desk. The intercom. Dialed 30. He was right: Hervé answered instantly.

Monday, midnight

"Come on up," he said. Put the phone down. Stretched, with a huge creaking of the shoulder joints. At midnight, Hervé felt up to hearing confession from the whole population of Hell. A lot better than he felt after dinner, when he was completely knocked out, as people are who get up every day at six.

What a blessing, this friendship between him and Bertrand. Midnight, I've got something to tell you, come on up. And if it were two A.M. and you were getting me out of bed, same thing. The openness between them. The complementary meshing, the affection.

Bertrand the gentle, thin and fastidious in his velour suit, threadbare and indestructible like the man himself. The worried, the scrupulous. The man who would turn a thought over seven hundred and seventy-seven times in the hollow of his skull. The most reserved of men, now known even

19

among the wider public for the boldness of his positions. It was unbelievable. The radical of moral theology. For the fundamentalists, the devil: to hear them tell it, a gravedigger of tradition, a violent man—a real Protestant! Bertrand, who suffered so from the turmoil raised every month by his editorial in *Outlooks*. Who was floored by the attacks. Who you had to hold up bodily.

And his counterpart—Father Hervé Montgaroult, me—the fellow Bertrand called his bulwark. Physically sure, a rugby forward. But otherwise, not a single idea, not the slightest imagination. Capable at most of rehashing his course in cataphatic ontology, and of repeatedly setting about, then setting aside, his still-unwritten treatise on the subject.

"Come on in!" said Hervé loud and strong, just as Bertrand was about to knock.

He listened to his visitor without interrupting him, without making a move, and without his face showing a trace of his reactions.

Bertrand stopped talking. He had not let go of the six pages. Exhausted, he handed them to his friend.

Hervé did not take them. He gave his sweet, rugby-champ smile.

"Calm down," he said. "No proof of the existence of God has ever held up."

These proofs and their grandiose and ludicrous history, the succession, since man began to think, of his efforts to prove God—that was Hervé's domain.

Each year, in late March, springtime brought back that chapter and with it one of the great moments of his course. The students—80 percent of them future priests—would protest at first: What need was there of proofs? Happy age: they had just made the great plunge, leaving doubt behind them the way a diver lifts off the diving board. Someday the board was going to topple onto their heads. "So what?" they would always laugh. And then they would get caught up in the game, they would see the noble nature of the gamble by human intelligence to know God well enough to prove him.

Of course the proofs were no use, or not as proofs anymore. But as reflections on God, they went a long way. As answers, they could not suffice. As questions, they opened up some superb problematics.

Hervé stood up. Whenever he launched into a slightly learned disquisition he reverted to the peripatetic stroll.

"There are limits to reason; Kant established that once and for all. No reasoning, no theory, can demonstrate that God is—nor that He is not. Careful, though: we can, and should, know *what* God is. Otherwise, how would we distinguish Him from the devil? The idea of God is not contradictory."

He looked delighted. In his little three-by-four-meter lair, even more cluttered than Bertrand's, he reversed course at the end of every sentence and, at every comma, he had to swerve around some obstacle.

"Science, which proceeds by proofs, cannot move beyond the world of phenomena. The good Cardinal Newman said it—you won't get to God by a *smart syllogism.* How could a rational construction, which links known propositions into a logical sequence, possibly demonstrate the existence of an unknown object? How could it demonstrate its *non*existence? . . . And if a person claims to prove that God exists, or, similarly, claims to prove that He doesn't exist, it's not God he's talking about. It's about some faraway star, a physical or mathematical object like other objects. Not about the God who transcends space and time."

"Just read this!"

Bertrand stood up too. He was holding the manuscript in two hands before him, like an icon.

Hervé shook his head. "You're not listening to me. You're wrong. The story of proofs of God's existence through the centuries is the story of Sisyphus. In fact, there's cause to worry for our modern times, when Sisyphus has already given up at the bottom of the mountain."

He had pulled a thick book off the shelf and was looking through the table of contents.

"Read this instead!" Bertrand started up again.

"Here it is! You've got four main types of proof: there's Kant's 'moral' proof, which is actually a postulate; but before that come the proof-style proofs, which are supposed to be logically compelling. Listen to the gorgeous names: the 'cosmological' proofs, the 'teleological' proofs, and the 'ontological' proofs."

He laid his volume on an undiscernible surface on his loaded bookcase. He didn't need it.

"The cosmological family of arguments sees God as the first cause of the world. The teleological arguments make Him the supreme end. The ontological arguments look to neither the causality principle nor the finality principle: from the idea that the notion of God is innate in all men, it deduces the existence of God."

"I know," Bertrand cut in. "That's not what I'm talking about."

"Plato gives us the ontological: all things share in the eternal Ideas, which in turn share in the unique Idea, sovereign Good, original Beauty, and world Spirit.

"Aristotle proves God by the scientific method. He considers reality, and ponders its efficient and final cause.

"I'll skip ahead here. It's Kant I want to get to, and his masterly demonstration that the proofs of God's existence cannot be scientific.

"For Augustine, only an original and eternal Truth could explain the truths the human mind experiences. Only a divine Artist could explain the beauty of the world. Only the supreme Good fulfills man's aspiration to Beatitude.

"Anselm, the great Anselm of Canterbury: he bypasses both empirical experience and scientific method. You recall his ontological argument: man carries within him the idea of a perfect Being; because he is so imperfect, he cannot have got the idea on his own; thus the idea itself implies the existence of the Most Perfect. It's absolutely simple!"

"Just read!" moaned Bertrand.

He moaned for two hours. "Read what I've got here! You'll forget your fancy speeches the instant you do!"

It was as if Hervé didn't hear him.

But when, at two in the morning, the exasperated Bertrand told him, "I'm leaving. More to the point, I'm leaving you the proof, in black and white," and when the door had closed behind him, Hervé Montgaroult stopped short in the middle of his room, staggering—a great bear at the sight of fire. His eyes were on the brown envelope in the middle of his writing table.

He could no longer keep away. All his efforts for the past two hours to put off the hand-to-hand combat with the Angel, that great display of verbal magnetism he had from time to time almost got caught up in, had been possible only because of Bertrand's presence.

Now began for Hervé the night he was always to remember as his night of struggle with the proof.

Tuesday, 8:45 A.M.

Jean-Sébastien Fichart watched the lanky bean-pole on the far sidewalk of the boulevard des Invalides. Fichart had just come away from a fairly tough hour-long meeting with the special affairs adviser to the minister for economic cooperation, and he was mulling over the little marquis's final sibylline remarks when the sight of the big guy interrupted his train of thought in midphrase. It had become second nature with him to register at a glance whatever wasn't right in a scene, and of course especially characters who stood out from the crowd. This oddball was smiling—always disturbing, a smile. Ten seconds he walked with his arms spread wide, his head back, and his eyes shut. He was wearing a getup that made him hard to categorize. And God knows Fichart excelled at quick classification.

The big guy was unshaved and uncombed. Beneath his open, and far too short, raincoat he wore shapeless, unpressed gray trousers and a weird turtleneck sweater with horizontal green and red stripes, which could only have been hand-knitted.

Just now he was pressing his chest, left side, with his right hand. Fichart understood. He would have smiled himself if he were still capable of externalizing an emotion. There was nothing dangerous. The guy was crazy in love, that's what gave him that look. He must have a letter from his guiding star in the pocket over his heart, and he had to keep fingering it every couple of minutes.

Hervé was pressing the packet with his hand, through his raincoat. He could feel a sort of heat coming off it. For almost three hours now he had been wandering Paris in a state of pure bliss. He had come out at six o'clock, as the day broke—a day that was starting off fine and cool: he had the sensation he was stepping into the sea. Judging from the wet pavement, it must have rained. Hervé could not have said when. He felt as if he'd spent the night underground.

He had wandered about between Saint-Sulpice and Cambronne without thinking to check his watch. Time was no longer time. The few cars moved either very fast or very slowly through streets made vaster by the silence. Hervé could not decide whether he was profoundly calm or overexcited.

He who could, if necessary, stay locked up for two days straight without losing any of his body tone—and who had done it so often, to finish an article or restructure a class in response to some news event—seeing the night pale, he needed to go test in the great city his new consciousness of being in the world.

He was barely aware of walking. The future, the past, danced about him. Voices caressed him, a mass of voices broken loose from the days to come and echoing from the dawn of time.

Another few hours, perhaps a few days, and the millions of invisible sleepers around him, the billions of the dead and of children not yet born, would see their lives come clear.

God was no longer mysterious. Evil was no longer a mystery. God was no longer either heartbreaking or heartbroken, and the question that for centuries had woken men in the night would no longer arise, the hideous question of whether He had or had not a role in evil.

God was the Immeasurably Beautiful. God the Whole, abolishing duality and reconciling the irreconcilable. God the Festival, and no longer the spirit's torture. God the Light, bringing clarity to horror—and surely evil did not exist apart from Him: How could anything exist apart from God?

Hervé had gone down the rue de Sèvres twice. The second time, Paris was waking up. The cafés were opening. First the men, then the women, began to appear. Hervé felt like calling out to them, "There's no need! Stay home. Turn on the radio, the television. Wait!"

Believing was no longer an issue. The world was

intelligible. Ears heard: cacophony was gone from creation. Eyes saw: the universe, hitherto jumbled like a holographic drawing, now found its depth and meaning.

Around seven o'clock, Hervé sat down for a moment on a bench on rue Dupleix. A near-dwarf of a man, his cheeks blue with beard, was hauling in two garbage cans. Hervé was eager for him to *know*. What would it matter then that at sixty he was still a janitor as he'd been at twenty, and even more shrunken, and that he hadn't yet laid the first stone of his dream house back home, way down there in Portugal?

Nothing would change about his daily schedule. Yet everything would be different. Pedro would no longer labor in bitterness, but instead in the awareness of being—and having all his life been—in a necessary place, in the same way other people were. Neither more nor less. Necessary.

Two gentlemen went past in the rear of a limousine. Hervé gazed after them.

There would be no such thing as success any longer: Do the sea or the sky have success? No more failure: Does a tree know failure? No more hierarchy among men: Is the night superior to the river?

Edgar-Quinet, Montparnasse, Raspail—by eight-thirty, the boulevards had filled up. Hervé was still walking, without fatigue, or hunger, or thirst, stirred at the thought that these men and women, every one of them pale, every one of whom he wanted to take into his arms, were right then living through their last moments of loneliness.

In a few hours, a few days at most, these bruised people would come to know utter safety. What was digging at them this minute on the boulevard—the way he would say, "Paula, I do love you, *a lot*," and his look of finding the moment interminable; the why's, the unanswerable why's: Why him? Why at the age of ten? Why does a ten-year-old child die of cancer? Why mine? Why me?—all those torments would not disappear, but they would finally have a reason for being.

There was no suffering that was not suffered in God. Nothing was without Him; nothing was suffered that He did not suffer. In a few hours, no one would be alone anymore. Every person would be living in the jubilation of the knowledge, and the joy of knowing his life to be intimate to God and God intimate to his life.

Probably, for a time, everything would come to a halt. People wouldn't go to the office anymore. The children would be sent to school, but they'd stop along the way, caught up by great circles of orators in tears.

People would talk on sidewalks, in the Métro, at church doors. Ah, the priests wouldn't know where to start! People would talk for hours in the rain. Neighbors who had always eyed one another with suspicion would be talking to each other. Couples ten years separated would phone each other from distant places.

The post office would stay closed. There would be a notice on the gate: HALLELUJAH. On the other hand, the museums would never close again, nor the Métro, nor the public parks. The guards would never figure out where their caps had disappeared to.

For days it would feel like a kind of general strike, a huge drunken spree.

The bakers would bring everyone back to their senses. "We're at work, us here. You're hungry, we're baking bread. But our flour is almost all used up. Come down to earth! Everyone get back into position."

Thereupon things would return to order—to what used to seem the disorder of creation and would at last look clear and lovely. Many persons would not change their lives. Many would. Nothing would any longer be the way it had been, but nothing of what is would disappear. Man would know himself to be truly free.

Tuesday, 8:58 A.M.

The street facade of the "Casuistery" looked the same as always. No throngs at the door, no journalists with camera in hand. Hervé glanced at the time. He would have said noon, but it was only two minutes to nine. Bertrand could not have spoken to many people yet. First he would have to inform the hierarchy, and the hierarchy got into the office at nine.

Dominique was at his post, beneath the portico and behind his windowed door. At this hour neither the switchboard nor the comings and goings would keep him very busy; he was daydreaming, perhaps praying. He gave the newcomer his half greeting, that hesitant dip of the head and the slight smile that never made up for the anguish in his eyes.

Dominique. People knew him by his first name only. He must have been thirty by now, but he did not look it. He was almost simpleminded. Delicate-featured, tall and slender, he would have been a good-looking boy except for the self-doubt that burdened his every gesture. He had hoped to enter the Society of Casuists, but it did not admit him to its ranks. He was kept on, though. He stayed at the rue Madame center as porter/switchboard operator. He had been living there for ten years.

Everyone loved him. It would have distressed them all to call their attention to the deep, unconscious, general condescension trained on him.

Hervé pushed open the glass door: "Dominique . . ."

He sat down beside the porter. He was worn out all of a sudden. "Dominique, have you got a few minutes?"

The other nodded, alert.

Hervé drew the envelope from his raincoat, and from the envelope the packet: "Read that. I'll sit in for you at the switchboard. Show me how it works."

Dominique relaxed. "When it lights up here, you press there. You connect with each of the extensions by pushing in the button next to it. At this hour, it's quiet."

With the papers in his hand, he went over to sit on a chair in the corner of the cubicle. The window beside him looked onto the garden, pink with peonies on this late-May day.

Hervé stopped himself from watching the young man read. He held out for five minutes and turned around.

Dominique had the papers on his knees. He smiled at Hervé, with no other emotion. All anguish had vanished from his gaze. He wore the most beautiful human expression that ever was.

"How fortunate we are," he said simply.

"Yes," said Hervé. "I haven't slept all night. I just took a very long walk outside—at moments I broke into a run."

He changed tone: "At other moments I wept with remorse."

Dominique opened astonished eyes.

"I've doubted God so much," said Hervé. "Deep down, I've never believed I was loved. How can I say it? I always felt just *barely* adequate. In my family, I was the slow one of the litter. I would have homework over vacation. People helped me—my mother. I knew very well why. She didn't help the other kids. As a young man, I felt like an oaf. I had nothing special about me: no distinct talent, no passion. I wasn't an artist, or an athlete, or a real intellectual. That's what drew me, I think, to apply to enter the Society. Being a Casuist, that was good. It was special, it was strong. It wasn't *average*.

"Social connections helped get me admitted. My father was a well-known magistrate, you may know that.

"Once I was a Casuist, reality hit me hard. In this world of real intellectuals, I wasn't average anymore, I was poor. I set to work. Like a madman, out of hatred for myself and for my inadequacy. You may know this too—I have a treatise I've been working on, for ten years. I had to pick the hardest possible subject. I can't get through it.

"That is, I *couldn't* get through it. Because now I'm giving it up. Or to be more exact, it's giving me up. It left me early this morning. I'm free of it now: of that idea of inadequacy, of my self-hatred, of the infantile determination to prove, by myself and to myself, that I was *up to it.* Up to what? Average I am, and average I am beloved."

"People need books for understanding things," Dominique said gravely.

"Ah, Dominique! I wasn't writing to explain things. Or that was such a small part of it. What I claimed to be writing in my own way had already been written, and better."

He slapped himself on the chest, with a laugh.

"Okay, that's all in the past! My course I'll keep teaching. I haven't been working in vain. I know everyone else's ideas inside out!"

He realized suddenly that, after ten years, he had no idea where in the house Dominique lived.

"And what about you, Dominique? What will you do now?"

"What do you expect me to do? Look, somebody's ringing. I'll pick up. I don't sit around, you know, after nine o'clock."

Hervé broke his habit and took the elevator. His room was on the fifth floor. He always climbed the stairs, two by two. "Crazy kid!" old Father Morin would say, slightly opening his fourth-floor door as Hervé passed by, with a tone of "What a racket!"

This time, though, fatigue was making Hervé

sluggish. He was going to try to sleep for an hour. Impossible to remember what he was supposed to do this Tuesday. Strange: a real memory gap. No, not so surprising: it isn't every day that a person is irradiated the way Hervé was this past night.

But before sleeping he had to see Bertrand, talk to him, give him back the packet. Consider with him what would be the best means to inform the others. Notify the authorities.

Well, then—his schedule. Hervé might have an appointment way the devil off somewhere at nine o'clock; he should have his mind clear. He entered his room and at the far end saw Bertrand Beaulieu, who was standing at the window and who turned around at his entry.

"I was waiting for you," said Bertrand. "Did you read it? Your bed isn't mussed—where were you?"

They laughed, they hugged. They wept. For a long moment they were silent.

Suddenly Hervé bounded to his feet.

"Good heavens! I have no idea what I was supposed to be doing this morning! By this time, I've probably stood up a couple of people, I bet you!"

His datebook put him at ease. The eight-to-noon space was crossed out with a big X that meant serious worktime. Between twelve-thirty and one o'clock was written "Marie-Jeanne."

"Wide open. Look, we shouldn't delay about telling Le Dangeolet."

"I phoned him just before you came in. I had trouble getting in to see him this morning. He couldn't understand what I found so urgent. Anyhow, he's expecting us at half past twelve. Yes, I told him there would be two of us. I beg you, do come with me."

The provincial of the Society had his office in this same building, on the third floor across the garden. Hervé lay down and did not sleep. Bertrand tried to turn his mind to reading the latest Ivan Illich, which he was supposed to review for *Outlooks;* he read the first paragraph eighty times over. The two men met up by chance in the little peony garden at twenty past noon, and they climbed the stairs to their superior's office as slowly as they could manage.

Tuesday, 12:30 P.M.

Father Hubert Le Dangeolet was in excellent spirits this Tuesday. Actually, that was true every morning since his election and, on two days out of three, right through from morning till evening. His accession to the position of provincial six months earlier had thrilled him more than he admitted to himself. Even so, God knows he did congratulate himself, particularly when he woke. He would open his eyes, and he would remember: I am happy, *very* happy—why is that, again? Oh, of course: provincial. Hallelujah.

The telephone rang in front of him, on his big black-leather desk.

"Your twelve-thirty appointment is here," hummed Jean de Bizzi, the young cleric who was his secretary. "Father Montgaroult and Father Beaulieu."

Le Dangeolet had forgotten about them.

"Send them up," he said. "But be sure to remind them I have only a quarter of an hour."

Beaulieu and Montgaroult: Le Dangeolet had had both of them as professors in a previous life. Ah, the worthy servitors of scholarship and of the Society, he sentimentalized for fifteen seconds. The fine intellectuals, courageous, upright, ascetic. For six months now Hubert Le Dangeolet hadn't had an hour to spend on sustained reflection. He thought of the scholar-workhorses of the Society the way a university professor newly appointed to a government ministry thinks of his former colleagues who are still teachers, always telling them "You've got the best of it," and convinced of the opposite.

What could those two want from him? Beaulieu needed to get his provincial's imprimatur every month for the journal, but that was routine; well in advance the editor would drop off the collection of articles intended for an issue of *Outlooks,* and Le Dangeolet would have the bunch of them read over by little Bizzi, who was a wellspring of up-to-date scholarship and reliable doctrine.

"Come in!" said the provincial, surprised that no sound of conversation had preceded the knock on his door.

God, he thought immediately, when will You give me the courage to speak to Montgaroult about his clothes? Brotherly correction in the spirit of Saint Matthew demands it, and I don't dare.

You had to be a scion of good (and sizeable) family, and a fifty-year-old bachelor, to get yourself up with such—such what? Poor taste wasn't the word; taste didn't even enter into it. Montgaroult dressed with an utter unconcern for what he wore. If he'd pulled his clothes out of a closet completely at random in the dark, the result would be the same. What would you call that? A kind of *well-born anything-goes*? Because Montgaroult's thrift-shop leftovers were more or less what a young man of good family throws out at twenty, when a first love starts him dressing nicely. This time, good old Hervé had on a thirty-year-old pair of iron-gray pants and a shrimper's sweater, red and green, that his old nanny must have knit him for his seventeenth birthday.

"What?" said Le Dangeolet to Beaulieu, who was staring at him hard. "What did you just say?"

"I said God exists, Hubert. We've always believed it, but since yesterday, we have proof."

Later the provincial would recall—and would make clear to the authorities—that he had never wavered for a second.

It was hogwash. His first thought was, I'll just demonstrate the inanity of the idea right off—*fissa*. (From a father who'd been a general—commanding spahis in Algeria, Le Dangeolet had inherited a dozen Arab words it always pleased him to utilize, even *in petto*.) Second thought, in the next breath: So I've got another mental case on my hands.

Poor Beaulieu, so provocative, so vulnerable: he hadn't managed to withstand all those volleys they fired at him. He was fingering the packet, which he had set on Le Dangeolet's desk; with the motions

45

of a priest at the consecration, he pushed it toward his superior and could only repeat: "In the name of heaven, read this!"

But there was no question of that; Le Dangeolet had things to do. At one o'clock he was lunching with the president of the foreign affairs committee of the National Assembly; at three he was seeing Bérut, from Channel One, to work out how long he was expected to talk on the broadcast "Sexuality/Sexualities"; at four o'clock he had an appointment with Mahuzet, of the Mahuzet bank, who he'd been told had the means to get him into the Hoche Club.

And besides, Le Dangeolet *did not want* to read these sheets that Father Beaulieu was putting into his hands now, lying prostrate across his desk, or just about. He didn't even want to touch them. Later he'd analyze this recoil; for the moment he had the inspiration he required. For every problem, its committee.

"We'll have this text examined by our experts," he told Beaulieu, pushing the papers back at him. "In fact, Montgaroult, you're obviously not here by mere chance. Is there anyone more expert than you to take a sounding on this latest-born proof of the existence of God?"

But Hervé Montgaroult had read the document, and he was overwhelmed by it. God was manifest in it, he said. Whoever read those lines would be convinced instantly.

Two mental cases, noted Le Dangeolet. So the thing is catching, besides.

"Experts, why not?" sighed Beaulieu. "They'll come around like everybody else. But I beg you, do it fast. I won't be able to keep quiet for long."

Le Dangeolet was already tapping on his electronic phone book. He picked up his receiver and dialed a number.

"Michalet in Louvain, and Schmuckermann in Basel?" he asked Montgaroult before the other end answered. "That all right with you?"

"Very good. *The* Saint Anselm specialist, and the master on the theological problematic of verification. There's also Gründler in Munich."

"Two will do. But we do need two—Hello? Father Michalet?"

The committee-to-examine-the-proof was set up in six minutes. The two experts could be in Paris the next morning.

"That was unhoped for," said Le Dangeolet. He looked at his watch. "As for me, you haven't even held me up."

He stood. He sat back down.

"I needn't say that we've got to keep this matter strictly confidential. This document cannot be revealed under any circumstances. Can you imagine the risk involved if it became public at this stage?"

He did not explicitly say: Can you imagine if *the others*—the secular institution—got hold of it? He went on:

"Has either of you got a copy of these papers?"

Montgaroult shook his head no. Beaulieu stam-

47

mered, "No, how idiotic, I didn't think to make photocopies. My life has changed shape, all my methodical, cautious habits have deserted me. . . ."

"Excellent."

Le Dangeolet, the envelope in his hand, moved to the windowless wall of his office. He lifted away the icon of the Trinity and revealed a safe.

"This document won't leave the premises," he said.

He opened the safe and closed it again. "I'll have the experts go over it here. And if we do make it public, that will be from here."

He held the door for his colleagues and ushered them out before him with a courtesy that clearly signified "Let's get a move on!"

In the elevator, under the harsh light, Beaulieu and Montgaroult looked like hostages. Le Dangeolet would have to get hold of Thomas Blin in the afternoon. In fact, maybe Blin, antipsychiatry apostle though he was, would deem that under the circumstances, psychoanalysis wouldn't do the trick, and that treatment by medication was required. He would judge. But there was no time to lose, the two old dears needed professional help. A proof of the existence of God? And what next? Why not an apparition?

"I forgot," Bertrand Beaulieu said feebly, as again his superior held the door for him, this time onto the street. "Perhaps we should find out a little more about the person who sent me the proof? He lives outside Paris, in Massy-Palaiseau."

48

"Good idea," said Le Dangeolet. "Do you know how to find him?"

"He put his address and telephone on the top of his letter."

"Did you note them down?"

"Those six pages are engraved in my mind, the letterhead included."

"Go see the man, that will help you wait this out." The provincial waved good-bye. "I'm praying for you both. I'll call you tomorrow, after the committee meets."

Tuesday, 1:20 P.M.

Hervé Montgaroult was a good runner—in his race along the rue du Vieux-Colombier he nearly knocked down a cardboard column on the sidewalk advertising Dior's "Eau de Prix"—but he couldn't get to the Hôtel Lutétia before one-twenty. He no longer recalled why Marie-Jeanne had wanted to lunch with him. The appointed time, however, he did remember. He was thirty-five minutes late.

The grill was jam-packed. And with the mirrored walls multiplying the crowd endlessly, he lost more time looking for Marie-Jeanne. Finally he spotted her, standing, waving with both arms, one of which was lengthened by an Hermès scarf. He saw their mother, signaling that same way to one of her eight children in the mob scene of a Paris railroad station on some first day of vacation, or to their father, the prosecutor, as he arrived late for a movie.

Marie-Jeanne Bellard-Moyaux was a year older than her brother Hervé and never missed a chance to hold it over him. He liked her. They were the "babies" of the brood. That they were now past fifty made no difference. They looked as much alike as twins. But whereas his big Kundera-style physique was an asset for Hervé, the same build made Marie-Jeanne a kind of great horse in a pearl necklace. Hervé could not have said if his sister was an unhappy woman who had never allowed herself to think so, or a woman too spoiled to have much sensitivity. She did have a husband on the Conseil d'État,* who was serious in the worst sense of the term. And five mostly grown-up offspring, whom she governed by herself, as Jean-Cyrille Bellard-Moyaux understood only one approach to reality—a legal file.

Hervé sat down, flushed with emotion: "Marie-Jeanne," he said, "God exists."

"Discovering *that* is what made you so late?" his big sister exploded. "Listen, my friend, at two o'clock I'm seeing the headmaster at Stanislas School to find out if Étienne is getting into the science program; you have a half hour to pick out the furniture you want—I remind you that the list is eight pages long—so let's not waste time, okay? What are you eating?"

Of course, Hervé recalled now: the family were dividing up the furniture from the summer house on the Normandy coast. That was it, the purpose of the lunch. The least of his concerns now.

---

*The supreme court for administrative law and legislative consultation.

"Marie-Jeanne," he repeated, "*He exists.*"

His sister stared at him. "What's wrong with you? You're very odd. You haven't had a vision, I hope? I thought your order was too intellectual for that sort of thing."

"The revelation I've had, the whole world is going to have in a little while. Ah, Marie-Jeanne! We've never trusted God. We've never stopped reproaching Him for what we didn't understand in His creation, and calling 'a mystery'—at best—the things we reproached Him for: the mystery of evil at work in the world, the mystery of the Great Silence while the cries of the just man under torture rose up toward Him. And our prayers were infantile: we would ask God to amend His work. Deliver us from evil, protect us from this, save us from that, as if the divine plan had got fouled up. But the mystery is clearing and you'll see, the whole human race will see: we can only give thanks. The Almighty has made marvels for us—"

"Hervé," Marie-Jeanne cut in, "I've heard the same line every Sunday at Mass for the past fifty years. If that's your revelation, the world's going to be disappointed."

She called the waiter: "Bring us another rib steak, please."

Hervé paid no mind. "Tell me, can you keep a secret?"

"That depends. Anyhow, you just said the whole planet was going to be hearing about it."

"Keep it secret for forty-eight hours. By forty-eight hours from now, the world will be entering a new era. You know Bertrand Beaulieu?"

"The one who's in favor of abortion?"

"Don't exaggerate. But yes, him."

"What about him?"

"He gets a lot of mail, all kinds, some very good things, some jackass things. Over the past three or four years, someone—someone he figured was crazy—has sent him a dozen different demonstrations of God's existence, each one more outlandish than the one before. But last night, what arrived was the proof of the existence of God from the same unknown fellow; do you understand? *The proof.*"

Hervé interrupted himself: "Don't look at me like that! You look exactly the way Mama used to when I would complain I was sick on mornings there was a math quiz."

Tuesday, 5:45 P.M.

Bertrand Beaulieu saw the rue Chevrier street sign with relief. He was late. He never took the suburban RER train, and he had underestimated the time it would take to go from the Luxembourg station out to Massy. Then he got lost in the little town.

A huge weariness weighed down his steps. God may have wanted it to be a simple matter to reach the discoverer of the proof, but the devil certainly did his utmost to complicate things.

Good old Satan! The game was getting interesting for him. Men's eyes were going to open up. Everything was possible in this world, from the sublime to the vile; the Father agreed to it all. The Son would save men, if they wanted that. The Father was at stake in His creation. If creation be lost, He would be lost with it. If it should be saved, following Christ, the Father too would be saved. The Spirit was calling on man to cooperate in this work of redemption, but was leaving man freer than ever. The proof, like the imperfect proofs before it, enlightened human consciousness. But the proof this time enlightened it totally. Never before had man been so much in command. In imposing Himself, God was exposing Himself.

At around one-fifteen, trying the phone number graven in his memory, Father Beaulieu had found Mauduit at home. The voice seemed unlike the handwriting in the letter. The voice of a modest man. "I was expecting your call." Perhaps not so modest.

Mauduit was very eager to talk, but not just now: he had classes to teach in the early afternoon. A professor, yes, of physics and chemistry. At La Providence, in Verrières. Five-thirty? Fine, five-thirty.

Thirty-two rue Chevrier wasn't much to look at through its front gate. A quarry-stone bungalow in a treeless courtyard. There were three names on the mailbox, among them, handwritten, M. MAUDUIT. Bertrand pressed the doorbell alongside. It had begun to drizzle.

A door opened under an awning at the side of the house. The neighborhood swam in deep silence. Martin Mauduit introduced himself as he opened the gate. A small man in his sixties, frail and bald. His smile and his eyes, the assurance and joy in these features alone, recalled someone— Bertrand remembered whom almost instantly: Bishop Gaillot. The churchman about whom every French person, even his warmest supporters, had wondered in 1995 whether he was Saint Francis of Assisi or Narcissus.

Mauduit lived in two rooms a flight up. He led Beaulieu into a room whose furniture was mainly books; he lifted four or five of them off the only armchair.

He was disturbingly simple. He prepared a cup of Nescafé without asking Bertrand if he wanted it, and did not wait for questions to get right to the heart of the matter.

He had been a priest, in another diocese, in the provinces. To know God was his whole life. His only goal: to think Him, *to find Him through thought.* He felt he was born for that feat.

He had exhausted himself at it. He had lost— maybe not faith; he had never exactly had faith, since he required certitude—but anyhow a clear view of his ministry. In the night, obsessed, he became convinced that he must petition the Church for a reduction to layman status, and must search—do nothing but search. Ten times he thought he had succeeded.

"I sent you my demonstrations," he told Bertrand, "because—I don't know . . ." He smiled his marvelous smile: "It seemed to me you were searching too, in your own way, to approach God *through the intellect.*"

But each time, two days later, Mauduit would realize he was wrong.

"I thought I was going mad," he said. "I lived in total solitude, a solitude wholly devoted to that superhuman task. I wasn't the one setting the challenge, though! I was alone, yes, but alone in the Hand that held me. We were two. I cried out for help. I started to pray—or Someone put me on my knees. All I had left was that one last resort, which looked like a surrender and was the exact opposite: praying, praying my quest until I should be put on course, however long that took."

Mauduit had prayed for six weeks, day and night. He prayed with all his strength; he did nothing else. He slept on his knees. He no longer went out. He was unable to carry on his classes. His landlady would put a loaf of bread on his doormat in the morning. Soon enough it was clear that the only way out would be knowledge or death. He smiled: "Knowledge in either case."

Six weeks, one day, and two nights: and then came the illumination. The proof was given Mauduit as the Tablets of the Law were given Moses on Mount Sinai: probably dictated—he remembered nothing about it. One day at dawn after spending the night in prayer as he had the nights before it, he emerged from a dark swoon and, around him on the floor, found sheets of paper covered with his handwriting. They looked like notes taken at high speed, badly scrawled but clear. Mauduit had only to copy them over, without changing a word.

Wednesday, noon

PARIS,
Wednesday, May 26, 1999, noon

Father Le Dangeolet shut his office door on the fourth good-bye to the two experts, and in three strides was at his telephone. But instead of calling Beaulieu and Montgaroult as he had promised, he took the receiver off the hook and, in sequence, set it on the desk, his body in his armchair, and his chin on his two crossed hands.

He was most vexed. The last twenty-four hours had seen him move from blunt skepticism on this proof business to obligation: the irritating obligation to take the matter seriously.

To begin with, the night before, Beaulieu had recounted his visit with that Mauduit who had started the whole thing. (Beaulieu, calm, unequivocal, equally annoying.) And it had to be acknowledged that the revelation process conformed to the most reliable tradition. The path of trials and poverty, nighttime; faith during that night, despite everything, like the light gleaming deep in the forest; and then, with no forewarning, by grace—the dazzlement. Nothing to quarrel with there. Martin Mauduit could not be brushed aside like some ordinary crackpot.

And just now, in front of Le Dangeolet, the committee-to-examine-the-proof had pronounced the papers evidence of a second Revelation—and the way they did it!

The whole thing hadn't taken more than a quarter of an hour. Karl-Conrad Schmuckermann and Léon Michalet, both of them, upon learning why the provincial of France had called them in, showed the same derisive prejudgment. A proof of the existence of God! The same lip-smacking appetite.

It made them look alike, though they were as different from each other as two people could be: the one debonair, the Belgian, slightly plump, shrewd as a monkey; the other meticulous, with the air of a Swiss doctor. They were like a couple of university kids planning a hoax. When it came to speaking out as experts, a whole shared culture, training, method, vocabulary, made them far more alike than they were differentiated by the twenty or twenty-five years they might have lived before joining the Society of Casuists. We insist otherwise, and we're right to do so, Le Dangeolet thought at the sight of them, but we Casuists, we do all look alike.

He had set his colleagues down at his conference table, before the great picture window of his office, and had forced himself to appear absorbed in his mail for a moment.

Father Michalet had read the packet in three minutes and he had begun to weep tears of joy. Father Schmuckermann took the sheets from his hands, plunged into them in turn, and fell to his knees, ecstatic.

Watching them, Le Dangeolet thought of chapter eight of the three-volume *Knowing God* of his years in the novitiate: chapter eight, "Physiology of the Inspirational States."

He had had some trouble bringing his two colleagues back to a state where they could think normally. Both of them could only repeat: "This is the proof," "It's achieved," and marvel: "It's all so simple, and we were looking so far afield."

Schmuckermann! The winner by a knockout over Hans Küng in the famous controversy over "Paradigm and Falsification" in seventy-seven! And Michalet! Whose article on divine immutability in the *Lexikon für Theologie und Kirche* had sent the pope onto the ramparts! Schmuckermann and Michalet like infants, suddenly! "The proof is achieved." "Hallelujah!"

Le Dangeolet had thanked them, exhorted them to silence, and dismissed them, a bit abruptly, perhaps. He needed to be alone.

He would talk later to Beaulieu and Montgaroult. The telephone receiver, belly up, emitted a *beep-beep* that forbade concentration. Le Dangeolet set it in place, picked up, told de Bizzi that he was out to everyone, and settled back into his meditation posture.

He forced himself to look at the papers left lying on the conference table. He should have been drawn to them; he was fully aware of that. But he wasn't. He still had no desire to read them, to say the least. No desire to lose his reason. No desire to change his life. Too pleased with his afternoon program, a preview screening, in a private projection room at the Gaumont office on avenue de Neuilly, of *A Man, a Real One,* that film about Christ that promised to stir up a good debate.

He moved briskly to the big table, put the sheets back in their envelope, careful not to read anything on them, and shut the whole thing back into his safe.

What was this new Revelation, two thousand years after the first? A complete Revelation. An ultimate Revelation. And why this great light, if not to signify that the end of time was under way? Le Dangeolet was afraid of those six pages.

He sat down again. Eyes closed, he breathed deep. He was convinced. He refused to let himself be touched, his whole being rebelled at the idea of giving in, but he did have to admit that the proof was there. You don't fool four Casuists. Not four out of four.

"God exists," said Father Le Dangeolet softly, very slowly.

And there came to his mind a thought that within a few seconds swelled up and stirred, and then utterly took him over. A thought that was neither very mystical nor too spiritual: *We've won!*

Praise the Lord for thus glorifying the Society of Casuists! The Lord be praised for having chosen the Society to be the instrument of His Revelation to modern times!

Le Dangeolet smiled. A wondrous vision, he was notified discreetly by chapter eleven of *Knowing God*—"Typology of Visions." The provincial saw before him—in Rome, in the middle of his big office in the Campo dei Fiori—the general of the Casuists ruminating aloud: "Ask the Supreme Pontiff to announce the news to the world? . . . No. Actually, no. We'll leave that honor rather to . . . yes, to our dear Father Provincial of France. My friend, do not protest. . . ."

The dream stopped short. It was urgent to set up a management strategy on the proof, without which it would remain a dream.

Priority: absolute secrecy. Put Beaulieu, Montgaroult, Michalet, Schmuckermann, out of action for gabbing. And Mauduit, for heaven's sake!

Problem: that last fellow happened to be a former priest. This being the case, could the Society of Casuists legitimately outflank the Church hierarchy? True, it was the Casuists' Beaulieu who first authenticated the proof. But that proof had been given to a priest—a humble priest, a probably crazy priest of the regular church.

Solution: talk to the Society's general immediately.

Le Dangeolet picked up the telephone, told de Bizzi: "Get me Father Waldenhag right away," and returned to his meditation, his fingers this time joined at his lips.

It wouldn't be easy to constrain the five initiates to silence. Of course, one could make them swear to keep still—he'd already thought of that. But as Beaulieu said, that was asking the impossible of them.

Institutionalize them? That would be perfect. Except that getting someone institutionalized is very difficult, *in practice,* in a democracy: you've got to have a shrink, a police chief in your pocket, the families . . .

Too bad, lamented the son of General Le Dangeolet, that a provincial of the Society of Casuists can't simply arrest his subordinates for a few days.

The phone rang. De Bizzi, his tone offhand: "Father Waldenhag left on the ten-fifteen plane for Calgary, where he will arrive at about ten tonight, Paris time."

Wednesday, 12:30 P.M.

"Saint Agapet Center," said Dominique. "I'll connect you. . . . Saint Agapet Center . . . I'll connect you to his office. . . . Saint Agapet Center . . . He is not in Paris today. Tomorrow, yes. . . . Saint Agapet Center . . . I'll connect you. . . ."

At twelve-thirty, usually, he stopped. He would switch on the answering machine, which in his stead would say, "Call back at two o'clock," and go to lunch. On this Wednesday, he hesitated. He was feeling good at his post. The world came to him in this tide of self-satisfied, amused, intimidated, tense voices.

Dominique said, "I'll connect You," and it was the All-Present he was addressing. "This one is for You. . . . That one . . . I'll connect You."

He continued for a few moments more and finally got up. He no longer had a reason not to go to lunch, either.

PART TWO

The Politicians

Wednesday, 1:30 P.M.

It must have rained during the night: the Tuileries Gardens were muddy, and Jean-Cyrille Bellard-Moyaux saw his Weston Regent wingtips smear dreadfully. But for the first time in his life, finicky as he was, he didn't care.

Instead of lunching as usual at the Brasserie du Louvre, on the Palais Royal square—the restaurant nearest the Conseil d'État—JCBM had gone for a walk in the Tuileries.

The night before, around midnight, Marie-Jeanne had given him a detailed report on her conversation with her brother. She was worried about poor Hervé.

"Now that we have the proof, believing is no longer an issue," Hervé had told his sister. "The cruelty of the world and the goodness of God aren't contradictory anymore. Human errors, follies, atrocities, finally make sense. Atheism, agnosticism, skepticism: the words of modernity will become the words of the past."

"Didn't understand one single word," Marie-Jeanne was saying. "I made him go over it twice."

Hervé had described as like a bolt of love the effect on him of reading the proof—he said "the proof." He saw his life as two separate lives, the one he called "blind" and the other . . . "inspired" was his word.

"I'm worried that he's having a mystical experience," sighed Marie-Jeanne without lifting her eyes from the parka zipper she was mending. "For him, and for Father Beaulieu, the proof of the existence of God is achieved."

Why shouldn't Hervé have a mystical experience? Jean-Cyrille reasoned, listening to her. For a Casuist father to know God—what was wrong with that? Two Casuist fathers, even, plus a secular priest; why not? But that their inspiration should leave behind a *text,* a palpable and comprehensible object, within everyone's reach and soon to be handed over to the media: the business began to be alarming.

That was departing from private terrain. Moving into the public realm—or public turmoil.

Marie-Jeanne didn't seem concerned otherwise. She feels she's not hearing anything new, her spouse noted with irritation. She doesn't see how a thing that people have, after all, argued about for two thousand years can worry anyone.

On the other hand, Jean-Cyrille himself had instantly been *touched* by the news—not in his heart or his soul so much as in that organ peculiar to the best stewards of the republic, which is the seat of *l'état c'est moi.* The model civil servant in him felt personal responsibility for this matter. At the Conseil, in ninety-three, at the time the Islamic headscarves were starting to flap over France, he had given a good deal of thought to the notion of secularism. He was convinced that it was the touchy epicenter in a very unstable social equilibrium.

He walked across the Tuileries, absorbed in speculations. He would have been amazed to see the spring in his step.

"Entered Tuileries Gardens from Louvre end," Fichart had recorded. "Circled East Fountain, headed off under trees toward Pont de Solférino. But at steps up to bridge, turned back. Seems to be retracing steps.

"Pace uneven, sometimes rushed, sometimes slow; normal at times. Classy clothes. Neat, except for shoes. Height: short. Weight: slim. Complexion: bilious. Youthful figure for age around fifty-five. Probably high-level official. Unusual feature: talking to himself."

"Block-the-ti-dal-wave," Bellard-Moyaux kept mouthing unawares. If the proof got out, there would be waves, big ones. Have to head off the crest before it breaks.

Going to bed the night before, JCBM had told himself that the night would calm him down. But it had taken him hours to fall asleep. Marie-Jeanne was snoring gently, sprawled over the pillow to his right. She had the knack of producing that low-level hum that you wind up listening for, whereas you barricade yourself against a more outright snore.

At seven-thirty, sallow, Jean-Cyrille had phoned his brother-in-law Hervé. He saw him in person and found him very much changed.

Hervé smiled endlessly. Bad sign, the fixed smile. When a political figure wears one, he knows he's going to lose the election. A woman: she's decided to leave you. A son: he's failed his finals.

As to Hervé, he was dropping his life's work, that "Ontology" he had been working on for ten years. He expounded some hazy thesis to his brother-in-law about the self-loathing a person puts into a work, into a job, into action generally. He was just letting go. No more ambition, no more targets, no more program. His only life plan: what he called "the presence." And of course love. *Loooove.*

Jean-Cyrille was convinced. A turnaround like that was unmistakable. Angels in paradise don't do any work, as far as he knew. The Casuist society did have the proof of God's existence.

Bellard-Moyaux had several professional obligations this Wednesday morning, in particular the matter of the five Conseil archivists who had apparently for years been taking turns each working only a one-day week, so he went on to his office. His mind thoroughly elsewhere, he must have seemed odd to his interlocutors, whom he did not hear.

At noon he had asked his secretary to cancel his lunch, cancel all his afternoon appointments.

Since then he was walking in the Tuileries (with his collar caught—Fichart added this to his mental report—the loden coat thrown on in a hurry). He could see how, within a few weeks, the proof of God's existence could destroy the secular equilibrium. Because that equilibrium depends on the noncertainty of God's existence. The absence of proof of God's existence obliges respect for unbelievers; but the absence of proof of the nonexistence of God obliges respect for believers.

If the believers should see their convictions ratified—what an open door to fanaticism! What fury among the unbelievers!

Perhaps the words "atheism" and "agnosticism" would become meaningless, but surely not "liberty." Modern man would refuse to abandon his free will. For every hundred who kneeled, a hundred would stay on their feet.

And how would the Muslims react? If Bellard-Moyaux understood correctly, it was the Trinitarian God of the Christians who was manifesting His reality. That would mean Islam at bay worldwide, enormous demonstrations in France, the Republic shaken to its roots . . .

It was urgent to alert Interior. JCBM knew Panzani, the Ministry's Corsican staff director—they had been in the same class at the École Nationale d'Administration. Of course, they hadn't seen each other since those ENA days on rue des Saints-

Pères. Bellard-Moyaux had graduated near the top of the class, Panzani at the low end: one of those differences that separate you for life. Over the thirty years since, Jean-Cyrille toiled along without glory, in the shadows of his glorious department. Matteo Panzani, meanwhile, went into politics, played the Corsican card, got himself a patron— and when that patron, Zonza, was named minister of the interior, he put Panzani in charge of his staff.

Jean-Cyrille went off to cool his heels at the Ministry at a quarter to two. He couldn't wait for an appointment. He would waylay his schoolmate as he arrived: Matteo! The fellow would be chilly for a minute or two. But the news would overcome his resentment.

"Gets back to the Louvre fountain, turns around again," Fichart noted, "takes off in opposite direction toward Concorde. Speeds up. Then looks at watch, stops short, and does his best instead to walk slow."

Wednesday, 6:40 P.M.

The provincial of France of the Society of Casuists was walking about nervously in the Luxembourg Gardens. He had done nothing worthwhile all afternoon. Until, cutting his losses, he'd decided to go calm down in the fresh air.

It was hard enough having to wait till nine in the evening to get the father general on the phone. But worse, since noon Hubert Le Dangeolet had still not worked out a way to keep the five men who knew from wreck—from talking.

Institutionalize them? he began again for the thirtieth time. Impossible. Just get them hospitalized, then, in a regular medical facility? But how could he make them sick, or get them injured? Setting up some Polish-Romanian, pre-1989-style accident would also take a lot of organizing. And in the hospital, even if they're injured, people talk. A nurse hears that God really does exist and confides in a friend, a Catholic, who rushes off to bring the news to her priest—and then the Church is in on it.

No, Father Le Dangeolet thought again, what had to happen was to get them away, the five kooks.

What about sending them an announcement of the fake death of one of their number, a Czech or a Finn? With burial services a thousand kilometers away? The trouble is that often in cases like that, the person you've prematurely sent off *ad patres* manages to actually kick the bucket a couple of days later. Then you've got remorse. It's no fun, remorse.

Have the five of them invited to a symposium? Of course! Five intellectuals!

Le Dangeolet gave a sharp kick to an orphaned bucket. He'd have to act fast, people are never invited to a symposium on short notice. You're warned six months ahead so you can arrange to free the time, have trouble doing so, flirt back and forth for six or eight weeks—and the paper gets written in the airplane on the way.

And Father Waldenhag was soaring around up in the sky out of reach. In the best scenario, Le Dangeolet would have to wait another two hours, more likely three or four.

Returning home to rue Madame at seven-fifteen, he saw Dominique dart out of his den right behind him: "Father Le Dangeolet!" Father de Bizzi was looking everywhere for the provincial; he'd asked them to watch out at the switchboard for his return.

Dominique's tone was utterly detached. Lucky

Dominique, Le Dangeolet said to himself (two-tenths envy, eight-tenths condescension), nice and peaceful in his ignorance and his nonresponsibility. Simple spirit; if he only knew what his interlocutor had been keeping secret for thirty-six hours now!

Little Bizzi really was in a terrible state. The prime minister's office at the Matignon had phoned at five o'clock, at five-thirty, at six o'clock: it was absolutely urgent that he see the provincial.

"Do you know what it's about?" asked Le Dangeolet.

"They told me nothing. It seems to be confidential. You're supposed to call the prime minister's private secretariat at 01-45-55-12-49."

Le Dangeolet took the time to sit down at his desk, and rang the number. He reached a woman secretary, a ripe-and-reliable type, who immediately told him: "I'll put you through to the prime minister."

Wednesday, 10:15 P.M.

The two men had had themselves dropped off at the corner of rue Madame and rue Honoré-Chevalier. They walked in silence up rue Madame, and in the darkness they passed only a dog that paid them no attention. No one saw them stop at No. 42-bis.

Father Le Dangeolet sometimes confused the two door codes, but this evening he never hesitated: PRACTICALREASON at the carriageway, PUREREASON at the entrance to the building on the garden. Dim bulbs illuminated the elevator shaft at night; he did not turn on any other light. Followed by the shadow in a greatcoat who was with him, he tiptoed up to the third floor and, listening hard, turned the key to his office.

He closed the door as slowly as an unfaithful husband at daybreak. The hinges creaked and the sound, signaling the provincial's return, instantly caused two or three other doors in the house to open, the doors of colleagues waiting for some time to speak to their superior.

Le Dangeolet waved forward the shadow, who refused, so he entered first, lit the little bouillotte lamp on his desk, and returned to lock the never-locked door.

In the half light he led his visitor to the conference table, seated him, went to lower the blind at the window, lit another, equally small lamp on the big table, and repeated for the twelfth time, "I warn you, Mr. Prime Minister."

Jean-Charles Petitgrand had laid his coat carefully on the back of a chair. He sat turned toward the provincial, his legs crossed right over left, his hands joined too in the hollow of his lap, and only the very shiny tip of his right shoe indicating his impatience by the rhythmic motion driving it. He did not respond to Father Le Dangeolet's thirteenth warning but firmly and simultaneously lowered his eyelids, a sign that he was persisting in his request.

Le Dangeolet went to his safe, opened it, taking care that his back should shield the combination from Petitgrand's view, and took out the brown envelope. The handwriting on it looked to him even battier than at first view. How the devil can the devil write? Of course the provincial didn't believe in the Devil, with a capital *D* and horns and a forked tail, but you never knew—or rather, you didn't know anymore, things were moving fast these past two days, and in the general direction of reaffirming tradition, it seemed.

Le Dangeolet handed the envelope to the prime minister, who, ever imperturbable, set it on the table and changed his glasses.

The provincial returned to his desk. Without this time feigning concentration on his own papers, openly he watched Jean-Charles Petitgrand. He was not sorry to witness the expected subjugation of this cartoon prince.

Petitgrand had manipulated him like a master. This man, the most courteous Le Dangeolet had ever encountered, was also the only one who had ever worked such open blackmail on him.

They had met at Matignon, in the government chief's large office, between nine-thirty and ten that evening. The prime minister knew that the provincial of France of the Society of Casuists had in his safe the six-page proof of the existence of God.

Le Dangeolet was stupefied. "How did you—" he began.

Petitgrand had cut him off with a smile. "Contrary to certain rumors we allow to circulate, our intelligence services work quite well, Father."

And the prime minister wished to read the document.

Le Dangeolet should have stared in astonishment, played dumb. He lacked the habit, it didn't occur to him. "The matter is strictly religious," he said, very curt. "It concerns only the religious authorities."

The prime minister's smile turned disagreeable.

"We know whom that proof was revealed to. Needless to say, the man is under surveillance. We would have no difficulty whatever in obtaining the document directly from him. We are told that those who have read it know it word for word. It seemed to us more correct to ask you for it."

There was virtually nothing left for Le Dangeolet to do but negotiate his cooperation. He agreed on three conditions. Under no circumstances would the document leave his office, and no copy was to be made. The intelligence service would be severed from the affair; they were to call off their shadows. Last, and above all, the privilege of revealing to the world the proof of the existence of God would belong to the Society of Casuists, and to it alone.

Without further discussion, the prime minister had picked up his telephone.

"Etchéverry? Please contact the director of General Intelligence and ask him to drop the Father/Son/Ghost case immediately." A slight nod. "That's right."

Hanging up, Petitgrand had stood: "Well, Father, since we are now in agreement, will you take me to your office?"

"Right now?" Le Dangeolet had gotten up too, and regretted it. "I warn you, Mr. Prime Minister."

"I appreciate it, Father. Right now, yes. You do realize the issue here? My duty and my responsibility are at stake." He crinkled his eyelids. "And believe it or not, *I find this interesting!*" he added.

Those last words in a tone that made Le Dangeolet wonder, in fact, just why that interest and why such a hurry.

But after all, in acceding to so blunt a request, he would have his revenge. He was about to see Jean-Charles Petitgrand at grips with something more powerful than himself.

The prime minister did take a second pair of glasses from his pocket, but he hadn't put them on. He was utterly still, as if hypnotized by the envelope before him. He seemed incapable of moving on to the reading of the pages. Without glasses, he looked naked. Le Dangeolet held his breath.

Then Jean-Charles Petitgrand seemed to come back to life. His chin began to tremble. He slid from his chair and fell to his knees. He wept heavy sobs, his hands crossed on the table. "I believe," he hiccuped. "I did not believe. I was only a pharisee. I wouldn't have time enough left in my life to learn humility. . . . I believe," he began again. His nose poured.

Le Dangeolet rose to give him a handkerchief. Mystical trauma (chapter eight, footnote), a clear case.

Just then the telephone rang on the provincial's desk. A hellish shrill. Le Dangeolet rushed to it.

"Waldemar Waldenhag!" said a voice that was authority itself, from eight thousand kilometers away. "Father Le Dangeolet, you wanted to talk to me as soon as I arrived in Calgary. I'm calling you from the airport."

"Enormous thanks. Thank you. All right. Well . . . it's such a delicate matter. I would have liked to discuss it in person."

"Can you be in Chicago between nine and ten o'clock tomorrow morning? In Rome tomorrow night?"

"Can I . . . ? In Rome, yes, I think so."

"You sound disturbed, dear fellow. What is happening? Let's take a moment now. Try to tell me calmly what's bothering you."

"Actually, I'm not alone in my office."

"I do hear a sound, that's true. An odd sound, in fact. What is that?"

"Sobs from the prime . . . Human sobs."

"I see. Call me back at Saint Joseph House after . . . Just a minute. It's two-fifteen here, which makes it what for you? . . . Call me back after eleven by your watch. No later, I beg you. I have nine hours' time difference on my back—is that the way you say it?—and in the wrong direction."

Jean-Charles Petitgrand was no longer weeping, but he was the very image of affliction. He beat his breast softly, his eyes on a point in the provincial's office near the ceiling: to be precise, the shabbiest bit, between the two bookcases, of the plaster molding that, since his election, Father Le Dangeolet had regularly told himself he must absolutely get repainted.

Wednesday, 10:39 P.M.

Sanpiero Pieri was still at the corner, behind the wheel of the official Renault Safrane. Seeing the prime minister returning to the car together with the person he had heard referred to as "provincial," he switched off the classical-music station and stepped out of the car to open the back door to his employer.

What he saw stunned him. The government leader was gripping the elbows of the man from the provinces, he was gazing tenderly into his eyes. And suddenly he laid his head on the man's shoulder.

Pieri trembled for the Republic, felt hope for Corsica. His boss had meanwhile raised his head. The provincial turned and left. The prime minister watched him go, his eyes moist. He climbed into the Safrane and told the chauffeur, "Home, please."

But Pieri had not yet turned on the ignition when Petitgrand added, "We will be making a stop."

"Where, Mr. Prime Minister?"

"You can help me. I'd like to stop off at the first vicarage along the way."

"The first vicarage . . ." Pieri behaved as if he found that completely natural. He tried to recall the big bell towers in the area. "We can cut over to Saint Sulpice," he said. "It's right nearby. Otherwise you have Saint-Thomas-d'Aquin, on boulevard Saint-Germain. Then there's—"

"Fine, Saint-Thomas-d'Aquin," said Petitgrand. "Let me off at the vicarage. I won't be long." After a few seconds he added, "God willing."

He had to confess at once. An exception to his rule: for the past thirty years he went to confession once a year, the minimum prescribed for Catholics. But tonight was an emergency. The anxiety that had driven him so urgently to see the proof as soon as the interior minister told him of its existence: that doubt had grown into certainty—certain guilt, and heavy.

Pieri stopped the car across from Saint-Thomas-d'Aquin. The little square was empty.

"Do you see the vicarage?" asked Petitgrand, twisting his neck.

"Just a minute. I'll find it for you."

Pieri walked around the square. An insurance agent, the Office of Army Personnel, the Buildings Department of the City of Paris—but no vicarage. He climbed the stairs to the church door, scanned two or three notices there, and came back down four steps at a time.

"The vicarage isn't in the square here," he told

Petitgrand, "and I don't know where it is. But on the church door there's a little plaque that says AT NIGHT, FOR THE SACRAMENT OF THE SICK, RING AT NUMBER ONE RUE MONTALEMBERT."

The prime minister nodded. Absolution for the sick was just what this was about.

"Let's go," he whispered.

There was nothing to distinguish No. 1 rue Montalembert from the neighboring buildings, not even a sign.

"This is fine," Petitgrand said, though. "I'll go in alone. Don't leave."

The street door was open. But at the end of the entry hall was another door, this one furnished with both a key-code panel and an intercom for calling in to some twenty gentlemen. Petitgrand read down the names. Two thirds of them were preceded with the honorific indicating that these were priests. The others were probably priests too, but younger ones, or on the left—that is, opposed to any titles. Petitgrand saw no clear criterion for bothering any one of these sainted fellows rather than another, and he pushed the button labeled COMMUNITY.

For a moment he was afraid no one had heard him. But the door opened.

"Yes?" said a fifty-year-old in spectacles and a gray sweater. "Is this an emerg—" From the collapse of his voice it was clear that he had just recognized his interlocutor.

"Are you a priest?" asked the newcomer.

"Father Paindavoine, the curate of this parish."

"Father, I ardently desire to confess."

"This way," said the priest. "We have a small chapel on the ground floor."

He had regained his confidence. He was mistaken. This visitor couldn't be the prime minister. So humble, so contrite a man.

"This is why I've come," began Jean-Charles Petitgrand. "I have always considered myself a practicing Catholic." He paused. "A *very good* Catholic," he added sadly.

He had believed he believed, but he did not believe. Such was the intuition that gripped his heart from the moment he had learned that the proof of God's existence was achieved. He had held the proof in his hands, and the intuition turned to consternation. He, Petitgrand, a sincere believer and an irreproachable practicant, at bottom had not taken seriously the existence of God until this afternoon of his sixty-seven years. He had considered himself such a good Christian that never until now had he even thought of contrition. "And yet," said he, heartbroken, "apart from Sunday Mass, I was living neither more nor less as I would have lived if I were certain that God doesn't exist. As an atheist I would have been just as courteous, just as decent, concerned—a little—with social justice and—a lot—not to undercut the elite of the land . . . And, like Saint Thomas, for me to *take seriously* God's existence, I had to know the proof was actually established."

Father Paindavoine was disturbed.

"Would you please explain to me just what proof it is you're talking about?" he asked respectfully.

Petitgrand climbed back into the car freed of all anguish. Not only had he been absolved of his dreadful believer's unbelief, up till today, but he had also thought to confess his most recent sin, the shameful bluff that had got him access to the proof. He was pardoned for having made poor Le Dangeolet think that Intelligence knew everything; pardoned for having gone so far as to give orders, by telephone in front of the provincial, to cancel a surveillance that had never begun, to a phantom interlocutor—for there was no one at the other end of the line.

He had told all. The past was the past, and the present a new age.

Now Petitgrand remembered that the Casuists were all priests themselves. He could have confessed to Le Dangeolet. It hadn't occurred to him. Truth to tell, not for a minute had he seen Le Dangeolet as a priest.

"Avenue Henri-Martin now?" asked Sanpiero Pieri, who until this moment had respected his boss's silence, and had just seen the pear-shaped face smile in the rearview mirror.

"Yes, Pieri," the prime minister said kindly. "We're going home. I have one last stop to make still, but don't worry, it will be shorter than this one. Take me to rue Rembrandt, near the Parc Monceau."

Well! the driver thought. Something new. An address I don't know.

"Pass me the telephone," said Petitgrand. "Thanks." And an instant later: "Hello, Mimine? . . . I'm on my way home, yes. Just one person I have to see first, someone you know. What number rue Rembrandt is your nephew Beloeil? Benjamin, yes . . . Number Two. Good. And his telephone?"

Beloeil—the name sounded familiar to Pieri. But really, a nephew . . . Private-life-wise, this prime minister was not a lot of laughs.

Thereupon, Jean-Charles Petitgrand settled back comfortably into the rear seat of the big Renault sedan. He couldn't believe his body, his soul, his whole being: he was *happy*. His life was changing. What were the only truly bright moments he had known in the forty-four years since he graduated from the ENA? The only ones not riddled with power, the spirit of power, the maneuvers around power, the dreadful reflexes of powerful men? The moments when he was tending to his rosebushes out at Pontchartrain. Two or three mornings a year, in the summer. Far from the Court. Silence. The open air. Mimine not daring to believe he was actually devoting *several hours* to her, as stirred as she was in the early days of their marriage, rejuvenated . . .

And what *mattered,* now, in the life of Jean-Charles Petitgrand? What was he going to hold on to, among his activities, now that he *believed?* His roses. His wife and his roses. For the ten or fifteen years he had left to live, he would praise the Eternal One, simply, through love for his roses, for his wife, and for his fellow man, at Pontchartrain.

Wednesday, 10:57 P.M.

"What's that you said?" thundered Waldemar Waldenhag.

The telephone had trembled in the provincial's hand.

"Father Waldenhag," repeated Hubert Le Dangeolet, "we have the proof of the existence of God."

Concise, precise, he recounted the circumstances around the appearance of the proof. The general let him talk and declared, "That is impossible."

"It was possible for God to make Himself man. Why would it be impossible for Him to prove He exists?"

"Give me the gist of those pages."

"I cannot."

"How come?"

"I haven't read them."

"You can't mean that! Read them and then we'll talk."

"I can't. That is to say, I don't want to."

I'm afraid to, Le Dangeolet said to himself. That announcement is a sign that the end of time is near. And *I don't want it.* I don't want to die, I don't want the world to be over.

"It's my duty," he said aloud. "I've got to keep a cool head and a free mind. The people who have read the proof are immediately possessed by it. They no longer have the slightest objectivity. I've seen four of our colleagues topple over, one after the other. We can't have our whole Casuist province in France slipping into a way of life that is positively Franciscan, and the *ecstatic* branch at that."

"True."

"In fact I've just seen something odder still: one person—I'll tell you later who—converted by the proof without having read it, just at the mere sight of it. You'll agree that I cannot plunge in."

"I understand you. And basically I approve your decision," said Waldenhag dubiously. "I don't believe for a minute that the proof of God's existence is achieved. My faith prohibits me from believing that the proof of God's existence can ever be adduced. My God is not an object for verification, He is a subject for love. My faith is not knowledge, it is acceptance. It is a matter not of calculation but of trust."

His tone had grown dreamy, somewhat contradictory to his words. "Listen. Today is Wednesday. I'll be in Rome tomorrow evening. Meet me there with the document. We'll read it together."

112

"Right, there's no time to lose, actually. One of the five initiates has talked."

"You're sure?"

"The state authorities know about it—the top people do, anyhow. Guess who it was in my study a while ago keeping me from talking to you? The one who believed without having read—"

"Tell me."

"Our prime minister, Petitgrand. Central Intelligence is aware of it. I've done what I could to keep things secret, but I have no illusions. If we don't watch out, word will spread like a gunpowder trail. It's not the prime minister who worries me: he's a man who can see how explosive the information is. It's the five visionaries, our four colleagues here and Mauduit. Since noon today I've been racking my brain, looking for a way to keep them from talking, and I confess, Father Waldenhag, I'm unworthy of my office—*I haven't come up with a thing!* I've looked in all kinds of directions without finding anything good, I mean workable. All I could do was ask those poor God-filled wretches to keep quiet. They won't hold out for long."

"The simplest ideas are not always the least worthwhile ones. You leave for Rome as soon as possible with the document and the five initiates. Tell them I want to see them. When they get to Rome, I'll take charge."

Wednesday, 11:01 P.M.

And meanwhile, in his barren chamber, without a book, Dominique fell asleep over a prayer that came to him for the first time: "Let me not wake up tomorrow. I long so much to see You. Why make me wait? It is hard knowing You to be so near, and hidden. But if You prefer me to wake up tomorrow morning, let it be to feel as happy as I do tonight."

Thursday, 2:44 A.M.

Sanpiero Pieri turned toward the rear seat of the Renault sedan and seized Petitgrand by the wrist.

"Don't go in there, Mr. Prime Minister!"

But the prime minister would not listen. He had had himself driven in the middle of the night to The High Commissioner, the well-known gay nightclub. Pieri hadn't said a word. And now his employer had just told him, as if there was nothing to it, "You can go, my friend. I'll get home on my own."

Pieri felt released from the duty of silence.

"Mr. Prime Minister, you can't go into that kind of place!"

Petitgrand took it very badly: "You mind your own business, friend. My private life is my concern. Do I ask you who you sleep with? Anyhow, if you must know, I have an appointment at The High Commissioner with Benjamin Beloeil. . . ."

*   *   *

Pieri opened his eyes. He was sweating, turned around head to foot in his bed. It took him a long time to calm down. He had never slept with anyone; he loved his old mama too much. The prime minister was hetero, and probably faithful. As for Benjamin Beloeil . . . Suddenly it came back to Pieri. This Beloeil turned up on television on the slightest pretext. He ran some behavior-study institute; he knew before you did why you wouldn't be voting in the next election, that you were finished with boxer shorts and were going back to briefs, and to what degree you considered reincarnation compatible with bodily resurrection.

Thursday, 7:36 A.M.

Father Paindavoine knocked at the door of his first vicar. Adrien Forest opened the door wearing a silky deep-green dressing gown. His vocation had come late, and from a lengthy bachelorhood he still had several very good items of clothing. The two men broke into smiles at the same time. Both were thinking of Claire Henry-Duparc, formerly Forest, Adrien's sister. One day when a third vicar was looking in amusement at the elegantly threadbare rust-tweed jacket that Forest had put on for dinner, the latter felt constrained to say: "Well, I do have some obligation to wear my sister's gifts." Since then, at the vicarage, notable items from Father Forest's wardrobe were never described otherwise than as "gifts from Madame his sister."

"Adrien," said the senior priest, "could you do me a favor? I need you to deal with the architect from Historic Monuments I'm supposed to see at ten this morning. I suddenly have to go over to the archbishopric, and I worry I'll be there a long time."

Georges Paindavoine could not keep to himself what had been entrusted to him the night before. He had not slept badly, though; on the contrary. After the prime minister left, he was in turmoil for an hour. Then he made his decision and was relieved: he would carry his concerns directly to his bishop, who in his case was the archbishop of Paris. He wouldn't talk to anyone else. He was worried about tales spreading.

That wouldn't be betraying the secrecy of the confessional. What the prime minister had on his conscience Paindavoine wouldn't say a word about. He wouldn't divulge the visitor's identity. He would only talk about this proof the Casuists had apparently got their hands on.

Thursday, 10:02 A.M.

Hubert Le Dangeolet hung up, exasperated. He set his two hands flat on his desktop while he closed his eyes and breathed deep. Since nine in the morning he had been trying to get hold of the prime minister, and all of Matignon was blocking him.

It was a bit much. Petitgrand snapped his fingers, called him out at nine-thirty at night, at ten o'clock bent him to his whim. And then the next morning when Le Dangeolet had something to say to him, it was "Father Le Dangeolet? We've noted it, we'll get back to you." And nothing, no callback.

The provincial had reached the number-one secretary four times, and twice the chief of staff, who finally, a minute ago, had taken a lofty attitude: "You don't just bother the head of government like that."

But Le Dangeolet did have to see Petitgrand before he left. The night before, he had certainly asked the prime minister to keep the proof secret, but as something understood, without stressing it enough. He had to convince him of the absolute need for silence, and get a commitment to it.

And he had only a few hours left. He was taking off for Rome at 5:05.

He had been on the telephone for two hours by now. Between eight and nine he had managed to reach Beaulieu, Montgaroult, Mauduit, Michalet in Louvain, Schmuckermann in Basel: all five of them would be at his office on rue Madame at three o'clock, and by three-thirty at the latest they would leave in the Casuists' old Nevada station wagon for Charles de Gaulle airport at Roissy.

Le Dangeolet grabbed his electronic address book. He was determined to find someone who could get a call through to the prime minister before the morning was out.

Thursday, 10:05 A.M.

Thierry Martinmignon walked into Antoine Etchéverry's office at the *same moment* as he knocked. Never had he gone that far. He had an extremely strong sense of hierarchy. A chief of staff waits to enter the office of a staff director until the latter has said firmly and loudly, "Come in." But on this morning, he had trouble controlling himself. He sensed besides that Antoine Etchéverry had not noticed the faux pas. "Any news?" the director asked instantly. Martinmignon had to shake his head no. Not to be found.

They had telephoned everywhere—to his house, of course, his doctor, his daughters, his golf course, the offices of all the ministers. They were still at it; now they were phoning successively the head-quarters of all the national administrations—but they had to confess that nobody knew where the head of the government could possibly have got to.

Thursday, 10:07 A.M.

Marie-Michèle Petitgrand was aglow. She was arriving on her husband's arm at the Museum of French Romanticism. For the past ten years she had longed to visit this museum—she didn't want to go without Jean-Chat—and the place was even more enchanting than she had expected.

She felt she was dreaming. At eight this morning, his expression delighted, Jean-Charles had told her that he was devoting his morning to her. They had spent an hour-long breakfast over plans for this and that, the sort of breakfast you have in Italy, in the hotel. Jean-Charles had applauded the museum idea. Mimine grew bold. She couldn't bear the Matignon office and its ways. She had smiled, blushing: "If I dared . . . I'd like us to go there on the bus. . . ."

Thursday, 2:00 P.M.

The minister of justice's Citroën CX rolled through the gate of the Hôtel Matignon right behind the foreign minister's Peugeot 605, and at the prime minister's doorstep the two colleagues emerged from their cars some twenty seconds apart.

Very diplomatic-corps, Alban Dupont de Saint-Pli awaited Renaud Marasquin at the foot of the stairs.

"Greetings," Marasquin called, visibly affected by the gesture. And straight out, jutting his chin toward the handsome building: "So, do you know how many we'll be?"

They had known each other since the Lycée Carnot and a time when Dupont de Saint-Pli was still only Dupont.

"Not exactly, no," answered the diplomat. "But not more than a half dozen, as I understand it. I was told 'a very small cabinet meeting.' You have any idea what to expect?"

"No real idea, no. I was told 'very secret cabinet meeting.' But I do have a hypothesis. I have a feeling the June elections may not look so good."

The two friends left their coats in the vestibule and walked together down the corridor to the room for small meetings.

Jean-Charles Petitgrand stood waiting for them, and approached as they entered. He looked Marasquin in the eyes, a kindly smile on his lips, then graced him with an interminable embrace. He's been drinking, the minister of justice sensed, his nose in the leader's shoulder. A yard off, Dupont de Saint-Pli flinched unwittingly: the latest confidential poll from Intelligence is crushing, he thought; we're done for in the elections. He wanted to flee. He hated people to touch him. But he too was awarded a gaze brimming with love, and a woolly hug.

Petitgrand had always had ecclesiastical ways about him. For instance, when he was in deep thought, his habit of joining his long plump hands in front of his lips. Or if by chance he was recognized in the street, which always moved him, the sort of benediction wave he would give the onlookers from inside his car. But this time it was different. The man had changed. So stiff before; something had happened to him.

Marasquin and Dupont were not the first there. Two men were already in the room, talking quietly, arms crossed, at the end of the table farthest from the door, toward the garden: Zonza, the interior minister, and a fashion plate whom Dupont de Saint-Pli recognized with displeasure as Beloeil, from the Coxema consulting outfit—they had been at the Institute of Political Science together, and Beloeil never addressed his old classmate by any name but "Dupli de Saint-Pont."

Torrin, the minister of the economy, made his entrance. Petitgrand clasped him in turn. Torrin stiffened: *Good heavens, he's madly in love.*

The double door closed.

"Let's sit down," said Petitgrand. "We're all here."

Moving to the center of the table, he put Beloeil at his right, Zonza at his left, and pointed the three other ministers to their seats across from him. Everyone understood. The group was more than "small." Without Beloeil it would have been just family. The ministers present happened to be the only four in the government who belonged since its founding to the New Assemblage, Petitgrand's dead-centrist party.

The government leader was no longer smiling.

"Friends," he said, "I have brought you together in small committee—you, my close, my loyal associates—because the situation demands it. I do ask, moreover, the strictest secrecy about this meeting. What I have to tell you is going to convulse the country. And you are among the first to be informed."

Dupont-Dupli was falling apart: That's it, Intelligence says we're screwed. He thought of Cricket, his wife. Cricri cheated on him each time the NA lost the elections. She only loved him when he was in the government. Minister, in fact. If he were an undersecretary, she would turn her attentions to whoever had precedence over Alban in the order of protocol.

"In just a short time," Petitgrand was saying, "you are going to see life in a new light. My friends, the proof of the existence of God is achieved."

"What?" cried the three ministers facing him.

Neither Zonza nor Beloeil had blinked.

The three others belonged to that majority of Frenchmen who, if asked in a poll "Are you a believer? Practicing?" would answer no to "Practicing?" without splitting hairs, and to "Believer?" would start off by saying, "Wait a minute," then vacillate, then think of their grandma and answer, "Put yes."

"What is this business?" muttered Torrin.

"Are you serious?" said Marasquin

"What about secularism?" Torrin exclaimed. "This is a secular state!"

"Whether God exists or doesn't exist is no concern of the government," Marasquin added.

"And then of course, God . . . God—which God are you talking about?" sniffed Dupont of Foreign Affairs, as if to say, "Introduce Him properly."

His fingers interlaced, all benevolence, Petitgrand had let the squall pass without appearing offended by the breach of protocol. He raised his right hand.

"God exists," he said mildly. "God the Father, Son, and Holy Spirit of the Gospel has given proof of His

144

existence. That proof is for the moment being kept secret by the provincial of the Casuists of France, but how can we imagine that it will stay secret? It has made a different man of me, and a few days from now, all humankind will be changed by it."

"But what are you talking about?" Dupont cut in. "What does this proof consist of?"

Marasquin joined the chorus. "What's happened? After all, for two thousand years we've been told that God exists. What's new now?"

"A message has been sent to men," Petitgrand explained willingly, "a short text. You won't deny that a text can speak for God. The Gospels transformed the world, after the Tablets of the Law—not to speak of the Koran, the Upanishads. . . . Furthermore, in fact, if this text had to be compared to some founding element of the faith, I would sooner compare it to the Incarnation. It is primarily a presence, a clear, overwhelming presence—"

"I've got to see," grumbled Torrin.

"You *will* see, very soon," agreed Petitgrand. "But trust me enough for a few more days to believe without having seen. I have seen, and it's transformed me."

He glanced to the right, glanced to the left: "We three, who learned the news a little before you, we do understand your reservations: we had the same ones. But I did not bring you together this afternoon to convince you. You'll be convinced soon enough, along with all mankind. Meanwhile, you are in the government as I am. We will have the responsibility to manage the coming upheaval, at least the upheaval coming in France. The situation demands informed consideration. You know Benjamin Beloeil, from Coxema. I have asked Mr. Beloeil to give us a picture of what French society will become after the revelation of the proof of God's existence. Benjamin, we are listening."

Beloeil's eyes had brown circles down to the middle of his cheeks.

"I offer you two different projections," he began gloomily. "The first is for six months to a year, the other for five years. Within six months, within a year, we have to imagine France as one huge monastery. Everything that today is the motivating force of the advanced liberal societies—the spirit of enterprise, the quest for wealth, the concern for efficiency, the work ethic . . . briefly, what others might call the every-man-for-himself, the activism, the copycat greed, money as guiding light—at the announcement of the proof that God exists, all of that will no longer seem important to our fellow citizens. God becomes a *certainty* in our midst. How do we react? We spend all our time on Him. We just about cease to work. We earn much less money, but what does it matter? We no longer yearn to change apartments, go off on vacation, send our children to American business schools. We no longer chase after money. If we do work, it's just enough for what we need to eat and be clothed, to have a roof over our heads. Most of our time we spend meditating, praying. We study

Scripture. We succor the poor, we comfort the lonely. We gaze on nature. We feel we're opening our eyes for the first time. We breathe.

"Obviously, private businesses as well as public services are soon a shambles. Production collapses. The first effect of the proof of God's existence on society as a whole is an economic crisis without precedent.

"In terms of current indices, the country declines rapidly. The other countries probably decline too, but not all of them."

It's crazy, Marasquin noted, he's doing what Petitgrand does; unconsciously he's picking up all the stylistic tics of the Gospel.

"What about the non-Christian areas of the world?" Beloeil continued. "Peoples who reject our God, or even battle against Him? God only knows, that's for sure. Two possibilities: either God steps in and convinces them as well, or He doesn't step in, and there's enormous temptation for the enemies of the old Christian world to take advantage of its disarray to try to conquer it.

"In my second projection I'll get back to this vulnerability of France and the other Christian countries: their very weakness could actually provide the surge that ultimately helps them organize to survive.

"But meanwhile let's stay a little with the short term. How is the proof going to affect our institutions? What kind of government, what kind of law, what kind of justice system, is right for a society of people at prayer? What kind of army suits it? Of business structure? Of . . ."

The three ministers, still in shock, were no longer listening.

What about me, Marasquin was thinking, what becomes of me in this whole thing?

What will I have left in the scuffle? Torrin wondered.

I go under in this shitheap, Dupont had already decided.

I'm sunk, Marasquin foresaw. Torrin: I disappear.

Marasquin: My power as chief of the justice system is based on the unstanchable vitality of villainy, of fraud and violence, of contempt for laws. My function makes sense only in a world that's in the clutches of evil. In a world devoted to good, I no longer exist. With harmony established, what use is an enormous judicial apparatus, procedures, appeals and reversals, judges and prosecutors? Why have a minister? If there are still any justice officials at all, it will be ten or twelve of them off in a corner, administrators with some modest function, servitors far more than arbiters.

What makes for the power of the minister of the economy? Torrin ruminated. He controls the main economic forces of the country. He regulates, he authorizes or doesn't, he arbitrates. He makes rain or sunshine for the boards of banks and of nationalized industries, of businesses, and of the public sector. But monastic manufacturing—what does

he control there? What does he regulate in arti-
sanal cheesemaking, in workshops for weaving, for
fruit jellies, for herbal remedies? In a society that
has chosen frugality, I'm nothing.

"In the third place," Beloeil went on, "the effect on
people."

He inhaled deeply.

"We can predict that the effect will be inversely
proportional to the social weight of the individual.
And this for the paradoxical reason that in our society, the indispensable tasks are the ones least
respected these days, while prestige attaches to all
sorts of useless activities.

"I'll explain myself. The garbage collector,
the shoemaker, the truck farmer, all the little people
we can't do without, will lead more or less the same
lives as before. Like everyone else, they will render
unto the Creator the best portion, but their social
position won't suffer; on the contrary. Their work
will be more necessary than ever. They always
earned three cents, they'll still be earning three
cents, but now nobody else will expect to earn any
more than that.

"The same cannot be said of the big shots of the
world. What will become of the sports gods when
the spirit of competition has disappeared? The
automobile racers? The fashion models? The cham-
pagne heirs? The hosts of television game shows
that nobody will be watching anymore? The editors
at newsmagazines? The trend-spotters-in-chief at

fashion magazines? The genius inventors of triple-action fuel? The tranquilizer manufacturers? The directors of marketing, communications, public relations? *The director of Coxema?* Who will still pay for their trips and their cashmeres? What usefulness could they still claim, if they want to keep themselves fed? There's nothing they know how to do."

Dupont, the elegant Saint-Pli, was dripping with sweat. The minister of foreign affairs—what would become of him? What would he weigh on the international scene, the representative of a people on its knees? What am I, facing China, Iraq, Japan? I'm an African minister. How many divisions have I got? No more divisions? No more industries, no more exports? I've seen them, my African alter egos: at the UN, people get them mixed up. People call them "dear friend," and for good reason—nobody knows their names.

Beloeil talked for half an hour. When he stopped, he kept his eyes on his notes. The others also had their heads down.

"My friends," sounded the voice of Petitgrand, "please excuse me for cutting short your meditation. But the news will break any time now. You must be ready for it. Use this interval to advantage by considering, each in your own domain, what new arrangements will be needed."

He raised his hands to the level of his shoulders. "A world of harmony is about to come into

150

being," he ended. "Everything in our lives that was not in the service of God and His splendor will fall away like dead skin."

He had adopted a light, incantatory tone. "Gentlemen, you'll stay at your posts. Your functions will reshape and adjust on their own. The transition period will require resourcefulness, modesty. After which we shall vanish into the anonymity of the Good. The meeting is over."

Thursday, 2:42 P.M.

Father Paindavoine was hungry. It was past two-thirty, and since eight in the morning he had been chasing after the archbishop.

Between nine and ten the people at the archbishopric thought Monsignor Velter would be getting in soon, and would spend an hour or two at his desk before leaving around eleven for the colloquium of "nondimwit generals," as he called them himself ("Ethics and Strategy: Religions and Defense," at the Trianon Palace Hotel at Versailles), a colloquium which he was to close at noon.

So Father Paindavoine had waited, in a cheap, molded-plastic armchair, skimming without reading old issues of *Paris–Notre Dame* magazine. But at ten-fifteen, Monsignor Velter had phoned in from his car; he was just leaving the Fayard publishing house—a very interesting project Claude Durand had thought up; he would be stopping off at the clinic of the Brothers of Saint-John-of-God, on rue

Oudinot, where his old friend Masson, the China expert, was dying; from there he'd go directly to Versailles; he would be back at his office at about three; none of his appointments should be put off, no.

Georges Paindavoine had rushed out of the archbishopric to try his luck at rue Oudinot. He got there too late. Then at the Invalides station he took the train to Versailles, unaware that two different lines went to two different stations at Versailles: Versailles Right Bank and Versailles Left Bank. He landed at Left, whereas the colloquium was at Right. With the time it took him to find the bus that would carry him from Left to Right, wait for it, cross the town on it, and finish the trip on foot, he got to the Trianon Palace Hotel when the colloquium participants had already been at lunch for twenty minutes, and were finishing their vol-au-vent in Pornic sauce.

The meal would certainly last another hour. Paindavoine was uncomfortable at the idea of sitting down by himself at the hotel grill. He looked around the neighborhood. A desert with flowerbeds. No sign of a café nearby.

He came back to the Trianon Palace and he waited in the entry hall, his stomach hollow and an old issue of *Le Point* magazine on his knees, for the reopening of the doors to the dining room, where the generals and the archbishop were banqueting.

The archbishop emerged among the first, his manner somber. He had found the service slow, or the generals heavy. He was one of those people of whom the Anglo-Saxons say, "He doesn't suffer fools gladly"; it was a physical thing with him. Paindavoine asked him for two minutes in private. Not a second more, he read in Monsignor Velter's black eyes. He kept to the limit. In twenty words he had stated the problem. Important state official. Unrecognizable. Proof of the existence of God. Overpowering, apparently. Six pages.

"Nonsense!" interrupted the archbishop.

Pandavoine finished: "Something in the way the prime . . . my penitent talked about it makes me think not. Shouldn't we at least send someone over to the Casuists to look at the document?"

The archbishop cut in again: "The Casuists? What do the Casuists have to do with this business?"

It was quite simple, explained Paindavoine, they were the ones who had the proof in hand.

Monsignor Velter's tone changed: "Let's see now," he said. "I won't be alone going back to Paris. And my afternoon is full. Can you be at my office tonight at nine-thirty?"

Thursday, 2:45 P.M.

And meanwhile, at 42-bis, little Father de Bizzi was pushing open the door to the switchboard cubicle: "What's going on, Dominique? You're looking awfully happy these days. Did you win the lottery?"

Dominique looked at him, his eyes sparkling: "If you only knew what's happening to me . . . the best thing that can happen to a person."

Jean de Bizzi tightened his lips. Slim and dark, with his handsome head and his very short hair, he looked like a jealous child. "Really! Can I know?"

"Guess," said Dominique. "You have one try."

De Bizzi did not hesitate. "You've met the woman of your life."

Dominique burst into laughter. "Better than that! A thousand times better! Tomorrow morning you can try another answer, and tomorrow afternoon again. Careful, though! The third will be the last."

161

Thursday, 3:10 P.M.

Zonza had kept silent throughout the meeting, as if stunned by Beloeil's forecasts. Outside in the Matignon courtyard, the fresh air seemed to revive him. Petitgrand was walking Beloeil to his car. The three other ministers seemed reluctant to set off in their respective directions. Zonza signaled them that he had something to say to them.

Petitgrand was climbing back up the stairs to the door. He was, basically, at home. No sooner had he gone through the door than the four others formed a circle three feet from the steps.

"We can't leave it at that," roared Zonza, excitement triggering his Corsican accent. "The boss has snapped. There was no decision taken."

The others went further. "Let's continue the discussion."

"Start it, you mean."

"Whatever you say. But let's not wait till tomorrow."

"There's not a minute to waste."

"Where shall we get together?"

In one of their offices? Not awfully discreet. At somebody's house? Their homes were under guard, and photographers lay in wait there day and night. A café? That was risky.

There was a silence. Each of the four was thinking, Do the three others have a bachelor pad like I do? Which of them would have the courage to mention it?

"There's a possibility that . . ." began Zonza, looking uncomfortable.

He took the plunge. He had an only daughter of forty, a theatrical costume designer whose studio was a hundred yards from Matignon.

"Colomba?" cried Dupont and Torrin at the same time.

Paris-Match had devoted two pages to the beauty, six months earlier, reporting that of what was left of the left, she—ex-hippie, ex-leftist, and not a bit subdued—was the figure who most concerned the minister of the interior, and was probably the most thoroughly shadowed.

"Colomba, yes," said Zonza. "I hear she's in the United States these days with her company. Doing what, I wonder," he added as if to himself, "since the show is played from start to finish by nude actors."

He collected himself. "Her studio is a former stable, at the end of the Varenne mews. The concierge at Number Four has the key."

"Motion adopted," said Torrin.

"We don't go over there together," Dupont remarked.

"No," agreed Zonza. "Let's each of us go on his own. On foot. And we should be careful to enter the mews separately."

"Right now?"

"Within the next fifteen minutes. I'll go first. I will have unlocked the door."

Zonza actually believed he wouldn't get the key. The concierge at No. 4 looked at him cockeyed, and he didn't dare declare his title as France's top cop.

"I'm her father," he said. "Believe me, for Christ's sake. Apparently she looks like me."

The concierge pursed his lips. Zonza had grown very fat, what with the responsibilities, the big dinners.

"If only I recognized you," said the Cerberus. "There are plenty of guys hanging around by the studio. Sort of your type, actually. But you—you I've never seen."

"I'm telling you, I'm her father," snapped Zonza. "That's why you never see me around here! You know many girls that age who're willing to have their father hang around their lair?"

He finally did get the key, on the condition of returning it a half hour later. Torrin, Dupont, and Marasquin were sauntering around the mews, hands behind their backs, pretending not to know one another and as convincing at it as prisoners in a penitentiary yard.

The studio surprised them a little. Making the best of it, they took seats on two old hassocks and a sagging chaise longue amid dressmakers' dummies and costumes hanging pretty much everywhere.

"One thing is for sure," said Marasquin, moving right into the heart of the matter without preamble. "Petitgrand is dreaming, up there on his cloud. Harmony, my ass! It's chaos we're heading for!"

"He's dreaming because he plunged right into the proof," Zonza pointed out. "He's touched. From what I hear about the few careless folks who weren't watching their step any better than he was, this thing has a stunning effect. People instantly lose all perspective."

"God preserve us from falling into the trap," said Dupont. "There have to be a certain number of cool heads in charge. Things are going to start reeling."

"That's just it," said Zonza. "Things can't reel. There's no question of releasing this information the way they announce the weather in the morning."

"Within forty-eight hours it would be a heart attack to the economy," predicted Torrin.

"Anarchy," said Marasquin. "Religious fanatics don't like civil authority. They take their orders from higher up. Look at Iran, Algeria—"

"What about my Muslims?" groaned Zonza, suddenly very mother hen. "I'm minister of reli-gion-*s,* not of just one religion. If one of these religions has a victory, the others start festering. Confrontations break out. The country bursts into flames and fighting. That, together with whatever the police will be like—"

"In three weeks," said Dupont, "the Bonn conference will meet to lay down the foundations of European defense. If the danger hasn't been headed off before then, I'm calling in sick. What would I be bringing to Bonn in my briefcase, after the tidal wave? A nonviolent army? Generals in monks' robes?"

"To summarize," said Marasquin. "It would be rash to let the word get out. So the first priority is to keep it secret as long as no precise plan of action has been worked out. Who knows so far about the existence of the proof?"

"Four or five Casuists," counted Zonza. "The number-one visionary, a priest out in the suburbs by the name of Mauduit. The prime minister. Those people not only know about it, they're done for: they've read the document. A second circle knows without being overwhelmed. That includes us, along with Beloeil, a member of the Conseil d'État named Bellard-Moyaux who's close to the Casuists and who told the government about it, and my own staff director, Panzani."

"That whole little world has to be muzzled," Marasquin concluded.

"The second circle is safe," Zonza corrected. "And for a reason: no one's read the proof, we don't know what it consists of, and no one has access to it.

And then, everyone in that circle is as cautious as we are. I don't know what got into Petitgrand to hurl himself on the document. . . ."

"Very, very Catholic," Torrin guessed. "Must not have thought any danger could come from there."

"The ones who could set off the explosion," continued Zonza, "are the initiates in the first circle. Those are the people we've got to keep tight control over."

"Five, you counted, is that right?" asked Torrin.

"Six or seven. First, the chief—you saw him like I did—"

"I tremble to think of the country in his hands," Dupont cut in. "He still looks completely sane, but he's become unpredictable. There's nothing worse. If he were eating grasshoppers and honey, they'd institutionalize him. He wouldn't be the first one in the history of France. But the way he comes across, almost fine, we won't be able to do that. And he could strike the match anytime. For instance, it could happen that he decides to tell his superior at the Elysée. The president is allergic to cassocks, everybody knows that. He'll sound the alarm."

Zonza had been nosing about the studio for a few minutes. Finally he dug out a telephone from between two cushions.

"Panzani? Emergency, old boy. The prime minister is at Matignon, nobody knows for how long. Have him followed from the time he leaves. It's absolutely urgent. Let me know his every move, his every meeting when and as it happens. And meantime, figure out a way to get me his schedule in detail. You've got five minutes. I'll call you back."

The poor man was pouring sweat. He dropped onto one of the hassocks, which let off a cloud of dust.

"That's one almost under control. On to the next. The suburban priest, that's relatively simple. He's part of a hierarchy; we get the hierarchy to work on it. And the top echelons, to make extra sure. I'm very close pals with the archbishop."

He went to get the phone again, and this time brought it over to the group.

"Hello, Matteo? One more thing. Set up an appointment this afternoon with Archbishop Velter. Not easy? No, I know. Listen, if he really hasn't got even five minutes, ask him for a telephone appointment. Eleven o'clock, midnight, whatever he wants."

Zonza wiped his temples. "That's number two. Now for the Casuists . . ."

"We should have started with them," grumbled Torrin. "Put yourself in their shoes: What could possibly make them keep the proof on hold? It's the coup of the century for them, this thing. Apparently they're deliberating. What else could they be deliberating but the way to make the biggest possible noise around their scoop? We've got to watch out, a Caz deliberates fast. It would be worth our while to go feel out their father superior, and do it quick."

"They say 'provincial,' " Zonza pointed out.

"Provincial or not, that guy looks to me like the

key to the story. Petitgrand did say he has physical possession of the proof?"

"Torrin's right. Let's see that man. It's high time."

"Where do we find him?"

Zonza already had the receiver to his ear.

"Panzani? Tell me the address of the Casuists' provincial in Paris—that *is* rue Madame, right? . . . What number? . . . I'll call you back."

Thursday, 4:00 P.M.

Zonza had just gotten back to his car, prudently but very badly parked at the Bac-Varenne intersection, when his own telephone rang. Panzani:

"Now I can tell you, we were sweating it. When you asked me to put a tail on you-know-who, it was quarter of four. Well, that someone had left his office three minutes before."

Zonza paled. "Did you find him for me? Talk plainly, I'm alone in the car." Then, noticing that this was incorrect: "José, we're going to Forty-two-bis rue Madame."

"I called Martinmignon," Panzani said, "but that moron didn't want to tell me anything. Even though I claimed it was an emergency. Etchéverry, same story. 'Confidential destination, strict orders' . . . a couple of tombs."

"Did you find him or didn't you?"

"Don't worry, we've been following him for the past five minutes. But we had to pull it off with no help. We spotted him at Porte de Saint-Cloud. Traffic gets jammed up over there. You know Pieri, the prime minister's chauffeur: he can't stand to slow down. He set his flasher light and his emergency siren going. I'd already alerted the police before then. An officer in the area was intrigued by that big Renault Safrane suddenly dropping its anonymity, all the more because a minute after starting up, the siren stopped short. As if the driver was saying, 'I could force you to pull over but look, I'm not doing that.' Very strange. Anyhow, the officer recognized you-know-who. So it's in the works—an unmarked car is sticking right with him. The Safrane took the west autoroute; it just passed Sèvres."

"The west autoroute? Where in hell could he be going? Do you know the rest of his schedule? What's he supposed to do next, after this confidential escapade?"

"State secret. I wasn't able to drag a thing out of his people. I was annoyed. All I could get was a 'We'll let the prime minister know. He'll contact the minister of the interior as soon as he can.' But that sounded completely bogus. There's something I'm not getting. I don't understand."

Zonza understood only too well. "Above all, don't let him slip away. Wherever he goes, and especially if he stops, keep me informed. Matteo, you hear me: internal security is at stake here."

Thursday, 4:03 P.M.

Etchéverry had begun striding back and forth in his office. Right off, Martinmignon hadn't dared stay in his seat; he followed along clumsily.

"He came into my office," said Etchéverry. "You could have knocked me over with a feather; it was the first time since I'm working with him. He came over to me. I got up. He gripped me by the hand— I thought he was going to hug me. He said, 'I'm leaving.' I don't know what came over me; his tone was bizarre, I was scared, after our experience this morning. I asked, 'What do you mean?' His answer is imprinted in my memory: 'You've been handling things very well,' he said, 'go on that way. You'll handle them just as well without me.'

"A kind of reflex drove me to keep the conversation going, the way you're supposed to with a crazy person, you know, somebody who's suicidal. I go: 'When will I see you again, Mr. Prime Minister?' and he says, kindly: 'Someday, my dear fellow.'

"You'd told me the Casuist provincial was trying to get hold of him since nine in the morning. Out of the whole mass of the things he had to do, that was the only one I could think of to try to hold on to him: 'Father Le Dangeolet wants urgently to see you. I don't know what about, he won't talk to anyone but you.' His expression turned tender: 'Good man, Le Dangeolet. Send him my most brotherly regards in the Lord,' and he left."

Thursday, 4:22 P.M.

The four ministers met again under the arch at 42-bis rue Madame. "Let me do it," said Zonza.

Of the four of them, he was the only one people always recognized. He could be wearing the getup of one of his daughter's entertainers—people would still recognize him.

He pushed open the glass door to the switchboard booth. "We're here to see the father provincial."

"The father provincial . . ." repeated Dominique dreamily.

Zonza could not believe his eyes; this boy had no idea whom he was dealing with. "Can you announce"—he finished his phrase into the porter's ear—"a governmental delegation?"

Dominique pressed a key: "Jean," he said without excitement. "A governmental delegation to see Father Le Dangeolet . . . You heard correctly: a governmental delegation."

"That's enough, that's enough," muttered Zonza. The fellow seemed to be making fun of him.

"The father provincial's secretary is coming down," Dominique said politely.

Father de Bizzi was already crossing the little garden. "Mr. Minister," he greeted Zonza. And, seeing the other three behind him, choking: "Mr. Min . . . , Mr. . . . Mr. . . ."

The parlors for receiving visitors, on the ground floor of the Casuistery, were the size of a confessional. And de Bizzi could hardly ask the delegation to climb the stairs to the provincial's office only to tell them there that Father Le Dangeolet had left Paris. Thus he stopped among the peonies.

"This is most awkward," he said. "I was not told to expect your visit, and neither was the father provincial, I believe. . . ."

"No, indeed," said Zonza. "An unforeseen catastrophe."

"I'm very sorry: the father provincial has just left for the airport."

"Jesus Christ!" roared Zonza. "He took off? Where's he going?"

De Bizzi hesitated. He had orders to keep secret his superior's destination.

"This is a matter of internal security," Zonza burst out.

Dupont: "World peace."

Marasquin: "Public order."

Torrin: "Maintenance of purchasing power."

"Paris-Rome, the five-oh-five," gasped de Bizzi, like a martyr under torture.

It was 4:27.

"I'm heading out to the airport," said Zonza to his colleagues. "No point all of us going out there in a procession. I'll keep you informed."

"It's very serious?" asked de Bizzi, completely perked up.

"More serious than you could imagine," said Dupont. "Father, thank you for the confidence you've shown in us."

Zonza was already in his CX, his telephone in hand.

"Panzani? Three things, listen. First, the Paris-Rome plane, five-oh-five out of Roissy; I want you to hold it on the ground right now. Father Le Dangeolet, the Casuists' provincial, is supposed to get on that plane, and I have to talk to him before he leaves. I'm on my way to Roissy right now, but there's a chance I'll get there just barely in time—I'm at Saint-Germain this minute. So, second, you alert this Le Dangeolet—*e, t,* yes; two words: *Le—l, e,* separate word, *Dangeolet, e, t*—get him the message at the airport that he's expected in a private room, where I'll see him in a quarter of an hour . . . a bit more. He'll catch his plane, make sure to tell him that: it's being held for him. And third, Matteo: find me Fichart and send him right out to the airport on the double. He should see to it he gets on that Paris-Rome flight. The plane will wait for him too. Mission: not let Father Le Dange-olet out of his sight from the minute he reaches Rome till he gets back to Paris; keep us up on his slightest movement."

Thursday, 4:29 P.M.

Jean-Charles Petitgrand had fallen still before the *Yuki-San* tea rose, the glory and pride of the Melle-barre nurseries, at Saint-Cyr-l'École. To his right, the director of the rose garden was narrating the long genesis of that ineffable tea tone. To his left, two gardeners were nudging each other as they heard their boss muddle species and years.

Ten yards back of them, Didier Muchon—Inspector Muchon—was trying to look enthralled by the *Madame René Coty*'s at his feet.

Inspector Verjeau, meanwhile, was walking slowly back up the sand path. He would soon pass beyond the prime minister and his guides.

Thursday, 4:31 P.M.

". . . three, four, and five," Hubert Le Dangeolet counted off for the second time. He was herding the five initiates ahead of him along the circular hallway at Roissy–Charles de Gaulle airport—five innocents unconcerned about either the time or the possible jam at the ticket gate.

"Let's not dawdle," Le Dangeolet repeated. "Look, there's the Air France counter."

There weren't too many passengers bound for Rome: five or six of those men prefixed by *business* because they fulfilled a strict conformity of dress; two Italian nuns who had already recognized the newcomers for males they could speak to. Le Dangeolet arranged his little troop in the line and tried to calm down. For an hour now he had felt as if he were heading a bomb-setting commando unit, which any of a hundred unforeseen obstacles could unmask. In the airplane he would breathe again.

But when he presented the six tickets to the gate

attendant in blue, white, and red, the woman signaled to a monochrome policeman behind her. The man rounded the counter.

"Father Le Dangeolet? You're expected in the Garance Lounge."

"What do you mean, in the Garance Lounge? I'm leaving! I'm just boarding!"

"Your plane won't take off without you." The policeman dropped his voice. "The minister of the interior would like to see you before you leave."

Interior too! Le Dangeolet smelled some plot. They were going to gag him, go through his pockets, do him out of the great moment of his existence. On the other hand, he himself had been trying since early morning to get hold of the prime minister. He was departing very uneasy at not having managed that, and of leaving unsupervised a man in a state of near intoxication, the repository of a secret far too weighty for him and capable of turning the world upside down. An anxiety an interior minister would understand.

"I'll come," said Le Dangeolet. "But by no means will I come without my traveling companions. There are six of us."

The policeman was dancing from one foot to the other.

"Let's go," said the provincial, taking his arm and leading him off.

Thursday, 4:47 P.M.

Zonza burst beaming into the Garance Lounge. "Paris to Roissy in twenty minutes! Anybody beat that?"

He collapsed onto the caramel leather couch and, once there, seemed to register the presence of six gentlemen standing before him not beating that, and a policeman besides.

"Father Le Dangeolet," he declared to the six as he rose, "I'm very pleased to have caught you in flight."

"If I may correct you, Mr. Minister, you're keeping us on the ground," said the youngest and most corpulent of the six clerics, thereby giving Zonza to understand that he was the provincial. "Let's do this quickly. I'd never forgive myself if I were the reason the two hundred passengers on that plane missed the kickoff of the Rome-Paris game on television tonight."

Zonza had already drawn him toward the window. "I thought I'd find you alone. Those persons are . . . with you?"

"Colleagues," said Le Dangeolet, evasive. "Church delegations make up a not inconsiderable share of the air traffic to Rome, you know. What did you want to talk to me about, Mr. Minister?"

"Father, that . . . uh . . . document in your possession is of some concern to the government."

Le Dangeolet had gone green. "The government knows about it?"

"Some persons in the government. As for me, you should know that it was my people who first detected the . . . uh . . . the . . ."

Oh, yes, the provincial remembered, Intelligence. The not-so-dumb Intelligence service.

"I see with some relief," Zonza went on, "that you yourself are concerned not to spread the . . . the, uh . . . all over the place. Father, what are you going to Rome for? Are you planning to make the . . . thing known at the Vatican?"

"Good Lord!" said Le Dangeolet. "You can't mean it! Have you measured the consequences?"

"Have I measured them!" exclaimed Zonza, dropping the reins on his voice and his accent. "I do nothing *but* measure them! I measure, *we* measure, with horror, because all we can measure is how utterly we lack the instruments for measuring them!"

" 'The measure of love is loving without measure,' " quoted Father Schmuckermann of Basel, echoing from behind Zonza, his tone suave and his delivery Swiss.

The provincial and the minister resumed their discussion, lower, quicker.

Miracles actually do happen fairly often. The one that occurred at that moment will someday be authenticated by Rome. These two men, unacquainted five minutes earlier, concluded—afoot, and in no more or less time than it takes to say it— a treaty that was a model of simplicity, rigor, and parity.

They agreed utterly in the view that the proof was a tinderbox, and that the best thing for the time being was to keep it secret. The world turned into a huge monastery—no, Le Dangeolet confirmed it: God had never intended that. The provincial demanded the silence of the French governmental authorities in exchange for his own camp's renouncing any public disclosure for now. Zonza swore that nothing would leak from his side as long as the religious authorities kept quiet.

They decided to meet again, a week later to the day, and reexamine the treaty in view of what might have gone on meanwhile. They separated pleased with each other, and each very pleased with himself.

Thursday, 5:05 P.M.

Six fifty- or sixty-year-olds came on board. Jean-Sébastien Fichart hesitated: ill-dressed, fairly cheerful; researchers, probably.

Immediately the engines were started up and the passengers notified to fasten their seatbelts. Fichart looked at the time: it was five after five.

He couldn't understand it. He'd been sitting in the airplane for twelve minutes already—well located at the rear of the tourist section—and he hadn't seen among the last arrivals one person who matched the description of Le Dangeolet. Yet there weren't many latecomers. An Italian *mamma* furious because her eight- and ten-year-old sons had got on the plane without her—who was holding the ticket (the whole planeload was put in the picture) and who had been looking for the *bambini* for an hour. Two girls in black. The six baldies. Would the plane be taking off without waiting for the provincial?

Things were getting off to a bad start. Fichart

would have to examine the passengers one by one. Always tough, that business. The flight attendants were quick to spot you and ask you to sit down. You had to claim urinary problems.

And indeed, an attendant was leaning over Fichart.

"Monsieur Tonnelier? You have a message from the Opéra administration."

"Thank you," said Fichart.

His passport, this Thursday, was in the name of Hector Tonnelier, impresario.

The message was two lines long: "Five violinists will be traveling with the tenor, it turns out. Take all six in hand. Bonus commensurate."

PART THREE

Rome

Thursday, 7:30 P.M.

ROME,
Thursday, 7:30 P.M.

"Let's sit down," said Waldemar Waldenhag, showing the six Frenchmen to the ring of Empire armchairs in the center of his large office.

The father-general of the Society of Casuists was one of those men in whose presence one immediately thinks, It will all work out. Waldenhag himself had something Empire about him. A conspicuous density of thought, of bone, of heart. Beyond that, a very dark complexion, impressive shoulders and calmness, and a Liechtenstein accent you could cut with a knife.

He had traveled fifteen thousand kilometers in two days, and accumulated such a complex knitwork of scheduling that when he set foot in Rome an hour earlier, he decided it was simpler not to give it another thought. At eight-thirty, he would be opening the debate "God's Right, Men's Rights" at the Pontifical Institute. He had scarcely a half hour to give the newcomers, and half of that he intended to save for a tête-à-tête with Mauduit. But none of that was apparent to his interlocutors.

The general looked at each of the six men in turn. After which he smiled.

"What difference does it make, basically, to have proof of God's existence?"

Le Dangeolet assumed both an exasperated look and the prerogative of response: "Father Waldenhag, is this really a time to joke? I beg you! It's a serious moment, and there's no question of divulging the proof before we examine all the effects that act could have on the world. Because one thing is certain: the world will be overwhelmed by it. And there's another thing too that's far less certain: that we stand to gain all that much by it.

"There's no time to lose. I don't know how it happened, but certain people in Paris are aware of the existence of the proof. Thank God, these aren't journalists, they're members of the government, or just about. Their sense of the State should keep them from talking all over the place. But anyhow, the information is out. If we want to stop it in its tracks, we've got to act very quickly.

"I just had a talk with our minister of the interior. My traveling companions here were witness to it—the poor fellow hadn't managed to see me before we left, and he moved heaven and earth to hold me up on the ground at the airport before the plane took off. He was absolutely determined to talk to me.

"The government is terribly upset to learn that

the proof is established. And still more to imagine it broadcast. It has put its experts to work to get an idea of what could become of our societies once they're informed of the matter. The predictions are alarming. The first effect would obviously be chaos.

"Our complex, fragile economies will be turned upside down. Dazzled by God, men will have no further reason to keep working to make the machine turn the way it used to. The primacy of economic matters will crumble. Ninety percent of human undertakings will look foolish, meaningless, pathetic. The ad man, the beautician, all the merchants of dreams and escape, will close up shop. The arms merchants all the more so. The only tenable behavior will be more or less what contemplatives do: prayer and frugality. I don't see research in general, and theology in particular, retaining the slightest importance any longer, my dear colleagues. An archaic economy will develop. Suddenly money changers will close down, and stock exchanges throughout the world, and university chairs in international finance, and business schools. Frugality and prayer.

"We've had a hard enough time putting a little order on earth over twenty centuries. And that order will be undermined at the roots! The order of priorities, the scale of importance, the distinction between essential and incidental . . . The basic values of the model societies here below will come unbolted: values of work, of enrichment/development, of social organization. Finished, the acceptance of authority! Done for, the respect for hierarchies!

"In the longer run, a world dedicated to the good is not a reassuring one. I can understand that the paradox would shock you. But do you really believe that a world of praying people would be livable? I repeat the minister's expression, which he borrowed in turn from the experts at Matignon: 'We have to imagine France turned into one huge monastery.' France, and Italy, and Liechtenstein, and the others. We won't even talk about the consequences for demography: that could solve the problem by the extinction of the human species. No, let's suppose that the world does survive. We've thundered enough against the spirit of money and social exclusion; no one can accuse us of knuckling under. But from there to throwing out the baby with the bathwater . . . Mankind hasn't done so badly, with electricity, vaccines, nuclear science—let's admit it, even the atomic bomb. Some rye seed always gets in with the good grain, *inextricably,* and overall we've come pretty close to a balance. It worked. Why try to unbalance everything?

"The good, the pure good—we know where that leads. We've seen them at work, the idealistic communities, the Cathars, the Waldensians, the Anabaptists at Munster. Sooner or later, sectarianism takes over, with fanaticism, the withdrawal from reality, the temptation to suicide. The rejection of life and its ambiguity, all its fecund ambiguity, leads—excuse the tautology—to a preference for death.

212

"Believe me, this proof is loaded with danger. An angel has flown over: Can we be sure it's not the Exterminating Angel?"

It didn't take the five initiates long to break out of the respectful attention customary when a provincial speaks. At Le Dangeolet's first expression of doubt as to the beneficial nature of the proof, they looked startled. At the prospect of suppressing the news—stunned. The prediction of social chaos and economic regression had them frowning. But when the tone rose, swerving unmistakably to the tone of a prosecution—at that, in concert, the five began to reel through the classic signs of refusal: the moist-sounding *tsk-tsk,* the shake of the head, the index finger moving back and forth like a metronome, and finally the outright "What next?"

Waldenhag had gestured for silence from the orchestra. Le Dangeolet was up to the Apocalypse. Mauduit, Schmuckermann, and Beaulieu were displaying the ten variants on affliction, ranging from reproach to compassion. Montgaroult seemed neither more nor less dismayed. Michalet was beyond that: he was gripping his sides, literally, with his head lowered to hide his uncontrollable hilarity.

Hubert Le Dangeolet's last lines, likening the proof to the Exterminating Angel in a style only barely interrogative, detonated five sharp "Oh!"s.

Father Waldenhag turned to the emitters. "A dissenting view?"

It was a chorus. An opera, rather. The five outraged clerics were experienced at disputation, and too much in agreement this evening to let any one word obscure another. The responses pealed forth in quick sequence, like Mozart:

"Why fear a total upset?"

"The proof isn't revolution!"

"Apart from the shock, at its arrival."

"A few days . . ."

"The world's not going to stop turning."

"Of course, everything will live out differently."

"It's a matter of lighting."

"Of luminosity."

"But nothing will be really different."

"Nothing will be canceled out of the world."

"One would think, Father Le Dangeolet, that you were talking about some other text!"

"What is that idea about Pure Good?"

"The earth isn't heaven."

"It's Totality."

"God isn't Ahura Mazda—not merely a God of the Good."

"He is All."

"Ah, dualism!"

"Such simplism!"

"Why think that uniformity will set in?"

"Evil will always be evil."

"And human liberty, liberty."

"God imposes Himself, which is to say He exposes Himself. He exposes Himself to the possibility of rejection."

"It's not Stalin."

"People who do want to devote themselves to the redemption of the All will be able to do that."

"As they always could."

"But those who prefer to refuse will be just as free to do that."

"Freer, even."

"The cynic can be still more cynical, if he wants."

"The brute still more brutal."

"Making use, so to speak, of Christ's sacrifice."

"The proof can improve the world."

"It can also increase its tensions."

"The most likely thing is that it won't change much."

Now it was Hubert Le Dangeolet's turn to look astounded.

"Unbelievable! You think telling the world about the proof of God's existence will have no effect!"

"We didn't say that. It will lift both human consciousness and human liberty to their highest level."

"And that's all? Nothing more positive than that? I can't follow you. When *everyone* comes to know that God exists, and who He is, how can you imagine that the Evil One will still have a grip on men? That they'll be as lost as they are today, not to say blind? As covetous, as cowardly? That they'll go on fearing death as much as they do? Idolizing power, glory, wealth?"

The light of the setting sun bathed the room. Through the open window, beyond the balustrade, the pavement of tile roofs conjugated the whole range of oranges, of pinks.

"It's late," said Waldemar Waldenhag. "I haven't much time this evening, we won't finish. You have done me the honor of asking my counsel. Now let me consult the Holy Spirit. I must examine the dossier beforehand. I shall see Father Mauduit first, alone. Then tomorrow I'll see each of you in private, one after the other. You will stay at Corso Vittorio Emmanuele. Tomorrow morning at about eight, each of you will be told the time of your appointment."

He rose. The others too.

"Father Le Dangeolet has kindly brought me this proof that excites you so," the general went on. "Pray for me and with me. I humbly wish you good night."

He had shown Mauduit to one of the chairs. At the door he stopped the provincial:

"I will be at the Pontifical Institute from eight-thirty to eleven tonight. May I see you afterwards? If it is no trouble, I will meet you here at eleven-thirty. Ring downstairs, and tell them you have an appointment with me. It won't surprise anyone. I've had occasion to make appointments much later than that."

Thursday, 10:00 P.M.

"Father Paindavoine, I thank you," said Archbishop Velter. A thrill of gratitude came through his
handclasp. "I will keep you informed," the prelate
concluded.

He closed his door again. His office was lighted
only in the sitting-room corner, where the conversation had taken place, but he had no wish to illu-
minate the whole space, and he moved to the
window. He felt a swell of satisfaction as he went.
He had got the good Paindavoine to report almost
word for word the confession of the anonymous
big shot. The proof was definitely in the hands of
the Casuists, and right nearby: on rue Madame.

But when the archbishop reached the window,
all his contentment fled. What he now saw chilled
his spine. It hadn't been entirely plain during the
conversation, but it was growing clear at top speed:
this proof was the end of the Church of Rome.

Archbishop Velter was not in the habit of dodging harsh questions. And the question now arose bluntly: What does this business mean for me and my Church?

At first, certainly, it meant we had won. It was confirmation of what the Church had upheld unflinchingly in the face of rationalism, scientism, atheism, Freudianism, Marxism, structuralism.

But soon we would be finished. Catholics would, de facto, become Protestants: they would be in direct contact with the Father, they would use no intermediary. The clergy would lose its power. The Trinitarian arrangement would become comprehensible, there would be no more need to explain the inexplicable: it meant the end of theology. The end of the doctrinal monopoly on heavenly matters.

There was a graver issue. From the moment God was *sure,* in both senses of the term—certain, and absolutely trustworthy—and when, moreover, he was sure for *everyone,* man would become terrifyingly free. The archbishop did not delude himself. If man had stayed more or less moral right up until the end of this second millennium, there were two reasons for it. Either he didn't believe in God, and felt responsible himself for the world; or else he did believe in God, but without being sure, and therefore did good in order to make God exist, as it were.

But once he knew God was a certainty, he would feel no further responsibility for either the salvation of the world or the divine advent.

Archbishop Velter looked at his watch. Ten twenty-five. He crossed the large office with his famous forceful stride, seized his telephone, and dialed the number of Father Le Dangeolet—the direct line.

De Bizzi picked up.

"The father provincial is not in Paris this evening," he said in angelic tones.

"Where can I reach him?"

"He is making a retreat in a place he's asked me to keep secret."

Too late, the archbishop fulminated. He's already in Rome, with his superior. "He's in Rome?"

"You'll understand if I respect his wish for silence."

"When will he be back?"

"In a few days."

"I'll wait."

But, far from waiting, no sooner had he hung up than he dialed the number of the motherhouse of the Casuists in Rome, on Corso Vittorio Emmanuele II:

"*Sono il segretario di Padre Le Dangeolet. Lo sto cercando, è da voi?*"*

"One moment, please" came the answer in perfect French. "He is in his room. Someone will get him for you."

"I beg you, don't do that. If he has already gone up, don't disturb him. We have a telephone appointment first thing in the morning. I'll wait till then."

If they had said, "He's right here, hold, please,"

---

*"This is Father Le Dangeolet's secretary. I'm looking for him. Is he there?"

Velter had planned his move: he would hang up. Le Dangeolet would call back to De Bizzi, who would deny he had phoned Rome and would not dare imagine—would imagine, but never dare voice the hypothesis aloud—that the practical joker might be the arch—.

A third time the prelate dialed a number. Air France information.

"What time is the next flight to Rome, please?"

He figured among the people close to the Holy Father. He went to the Vatican every week, on Mondays, but wanted to be sure the 7:00 A.M. flight was scheduled on Fridays as well. That was confirmed.

He was checking in his appointment book whether he could without too much damage cancel all his appointments for the next day when his telephone rang. Pasquale Zonza.

Great God, that's right. Supposed to call back between ten-thirty and eleven.

Zonza, who sounded worried, who made some incomprehensible allusion to "certain cases where the separation of Church and State no longer applied," made another to somebody named Mauduit, a priest unknown to the archbishop, and ended by saying (in a full-blown Corsican-patriot accent), "It would be better if I saw you in person, no? Can I stop by your office? Ten minutes."

Thursday, 10:47 P.M.

ROME,
Thursday, 10:47 P.M.

The Eternal City was delirious: Rome AC had beaten Paris Saint-Germain. The Corso Vittorio Emmanuele II was delirious. The bistro on the Corso from where Fichart was trying to phone Zonza was jammed with delirious Rome fans, and Fichart could barely hear.

"What street? I can't hear a thing."

Impossible to understand what Paris street Zonza's car was parked on. Anyway, it wasn't crucial. Fichart had rung the minister at the Ministry, at the Senate, at Chez René. He had finally reached the car, and in the car its driver.

"Whose?" he asked the guy. "No, not booze—*whose* house is he at?"

Impossible to find out whose house the minister had gone to at this late hour. Anyway, Fichart didn't care. What he wanted was to talk to his boss.

"How long? No, I'm asking how long he expected to stay with that person. Ten minutes?

Yes, I heard you: Ten minutes? And he just went up? Well, I'll call back in ten minutes. Tell him Fichart is trying to get hold of him, from the Opéra. No, not Ricard—Fichart! *F! I! C! H! . . .* "

Jean-Sébastien Fichart had fulfilled his contract for this evening and was not displeased with his work. After all, it wasn't so easy tailing six people at a time. To tell the truth, it hadn't been so hard.

The six men had gone together, in two taxis, from the airport at Fiumicino to the little Palazzo Pozzo, on Via Fornarina near the Campo dei Fiori. Three quarters of an hour later, five of them, still together, walked from the Palazzo Pozzo to 21, Corso Vittorio Emmanuele II, right nearby.

Not seeing them come back out, and since it was eight-thirty in the evening, Fichart had assumed that they were spending the night there. ISTITUTO RAGGI, said the sign at the door. Some kind of research center.

Fichart was heading back to the palazzo to look for the sixth guy when he saw him approach, his step uncertain, and go into the *istituto* himself.

Thereupon Fichart had sat down in the Presto, across the street, keeping one eye on the door at No. 21, the other on the television, where Rome was finishing off Paris Saint-Germain. Spaghetti was served by the portion—the small portion. But the Chianti went down easy. Fichart hated to be beaten. He therefore slipped—a skill he had—into the skin of a nameless Roman, and had a grand time.

It looked like the six researchers were definitely sleeping at the *istituto*. Fichart could contact Zonza.

The ten minutes had gone by; he dialed again. Once, twice. Finally he got through.

"Hello? You say he's not back down yet? But it's ten minutes. . . . Yes, sure, man, I know what ministers are like. Okay, I'll call back in five minutes. No, not Ricard, *Fichart*."

Thursday, 11:41 P.M.

Waldemar Waldenhag was late getting back to Via Fornarina. He rushed into the portico, calling out as he passed to old Father Alessio, who was guarding the house that evening: "My appointment already went up, I assume?"

The old man shook his head, and the general backtracked: "Not there?"

"Nobody."

"He's not coming," Waldenhag said to himself. He wasn't surprised. A few matters had distracted him during the debate at the Pontifical Institute, among them the premonition that the provincial was going to pull out later that evening. The poor fellow had such a dark concept of what life after the proof would be like. There was reason to fear he would do all he could to hold up the propagation of the news.

As much as he could . . . Waldenhag went back outdoors to await his colleague on the sidewalk.

Suddenly he darted off along Via del Pellegrino toward the Tiber. The night was dark. Shouts and car horns were still sounding from over by the Corso. The general ran.

He got to the Ponte Mazzini in three minutes and, as he had expected, saw Le Dangeolet midway across the bridge, leaning his two elbows on the parapet.

The provincial was holding his fists at his mouth. At the sound of footsteps approaching he turned his face, and he didn't look surprised, either.

"Give me those papers, friend," said Waldenhag.

"No. You'll read them. Then you'll no longer see the danger in releasing them into the world."

"What of it? Whatever comes from God can only be good."

"The more I think about it the more I think that message could easily not be from God. It would be genius on the devil's part. Imagine—torpedoing creation by throwing proof of the Creator's existence into it! Doubt about the existence of God was the only formula viable for mankind. People who wanted to believe could believe; those who preferred not to didn't have to. No greater certainty for the one than for the other. A mutual respect—except for the periods of certainty. Certainty, on whichever side, breeds fanaticism. That's not all it breeds, but it never fails to breed that. Look at the Crusaders, the Inquisitors, as well as the atheist revolutionaries: all of them slashed and burned and guillotined, completely confident they were doing the right thing. In the end, doubt is the only counterweight to human madness. It's reason, that's what doubt is."

Waldenhag leaned on the parapet beside him and said, "Mauduit is convinced that the proof will never put an end to doubt. He told me that this evening. To his mind, before the proof, we had all sorts of proofs that we didn't consider to be such: Christ, of course; the saints and all the marvelous beings; but also grace—the grace that's manifest a thousand ways in creatures and in creation, in a gesture, a face, a sky, a flowering meadow. . . . 'A room gilded with sunlight, you know, that's a proof in itself,' Mauduit said. And we didn't think they were anything special. Just as we never recognize our happiness, Mauduit says, until it's taken away from us."

"Those proofs he's talking about are nothing of the kind. *The* proof is an explosive of a whole other order of violence."

"Listen," said Waldenhag gently, "your invitation to caution is well founded. I second it. We should examine the document over and over again. We should study it, evaluate it. We should take all the time it needs, and leave the outcome wide open. You've started the process. Schmuckermann and Michalet are men of learning as well as faith. Let's go on with it."

Le Dangeolet was not straightening up. A great cloud covered the moon. The Tiber was black beneath the bridge.

"Allow me to remark on certain words you used a moment ago," said Waldenhag. "You speak of 'the proof.' You say doubt about God *was* the only liveable formula. That means you're convinced."

"If I weren't," hissed Le Dangeolet, "I would read the proof. I do in fact believe that this document is proof. I would even say—despite what I suggested two minutes ago—that it comes from God. And I am afraid."

"Afraid of what, great God? I heard your warning before dinner. The Exterminating Angel . . . you're going a bit far!"

"No, I'm not. If the proof does come from God, it is a sign that the end of time is near. You see, when Beaulieu and Montgaroult told me about the proof, I thought it was madness. Schmuckermann and Michalet, and probably Someone else, changed my mind. I was happy, then, I assure you: we had believed without seeing; now we were going to see, we had won. But rather quickly, I came to feel uneasy, and the feeling grew to anxiety, obsession. That proof heralds the end of the world."

"We can't rule that out, true."

"It's very simple. This is May of 1999. The proof will fling mankind into turmoil; earlier tonight I talked enough about how. The just will convert, the others will dig in their heels. And in the year 2000, the Creator will cut off creation. *Sufficit.*"

Waldenhag was still. And then, calmly: "That could well be, my friend. But if that should be the case, the two of us aren't going to head off the end of time. Besides, be practical: if you throw the packet into the water, Mauduit and the four others will put it together again word for word, from memory."

"We could ask them for secrecy. They did make a vow of obedience. We'd forget this whole story. We would breathe."

"You think so? Two thousand years ago, some other people thought they could be done with a certain Jesus by eliminating him. Christianity was born at Golgotha. If the proof comes from God, even if you sink it in a concrete block, it will come back again."

Two cars swept by on the bridge, their horns jammed. A voice shouted: *"Non è certo la serata per buttarsi in acqua, imbecilli!"**

"I'm totally with you on that!" Waldenhag said loudly. And with no transition, to Le Dangeolet: "Why not have trust, and consider, like those who've read the proof, that this is only one more step in Revelation? The ultimate step, doubtless, but in no way a kick into the anthill. It will light the world, not overturn it."

"I believe that that light—that enlightenment, rather—will change everything."

"It's possible that it will change everything, but not necessarily for the worse. You've heard the three forecasts from our initiated friends: the world could progress toward the Good; it could rip

---

*"This is no night to jump in the water, idiots!"

235

apart and go under; it could not really change. Forecasts which, I'd point out, apply today, but also applied yesterday, and always have applied. You've noticed, by the way, the calm in our five friends? Their joy?"

"They're saints. And besides, for them, actually, nothing is fundamentally different. But for the nonbelievers? For the great numbers of men today who have no special fondness for Christianity? Those people are going to kick up a huge ruckus."

"The proof will be a harsh blow for them, of course. But only slightly more than for the believers, you know. We have so little belief, we believers. We hope for so little from God. We take what suits us from our faith, and leave the rest behind. We live for so many other things. Father Le Dangeolet, that's enough now! Give me the papers!"

Le Dangeolet slumped against the parapet again. "You should have asked me before. I don't have them anymore."

Waldenhag did not miss a beat. "You're lying."

"I'm lying, yes." Le Dangeolet's tone was deeply weary. "Here. Take them."

He pulled an envelope from the inside pocket of his windbreaker without looking at it. "In God's hands now."

"Yes, indeed," said Waldenhag. "You did what you could; now let it be."

"Are you going to read those papers?"

"I'm going to try. Don't think it will be easy for me. I'm not a saint, either. I'd adapted to a certain looseness. And I worry as much as you do about losing myself. But I have a personal reason for reading this text. I want to know why, how, and in the name of what superior plan the good and all-powerful God of the Gospel lets nations tear each other's guts out, lets the earth crack open in the middle of cities, and lets children die of hunger. I've 'explained' it a thousand times, using those enormously sophisticated arguments inherited from Thomism that you know as well as I do, and I've done it with such assurance that I must have convinced people sometimes. But for me, the mystery of evil sticks in my craw."

He took Le Dangeolet by the arm.

"Come now, go sleep. I'll take you back. Let's meet tomorrow late in the morning, if you would. At my office? Or would you rather outdoors? Listen, I'll call you toward noon, when I've finished seeing Beaulieu, Montgaroult, Michalet, Schmuck, and probably Mauduit again."

Friday, 8:30 A.M.

PARIS,
Friday, May 28, 1999, 8:30 A.M.

Dominique ate his breakfast very quickly, and always last, so as to be alone at it. On this Friday, he found little Bizzi in the refectory, waiting for him at the end of a table. He recalled their game from the day before.

"Ready for your second try?" He had a hard time using *tu* with the Casuists, but they were unyielding, they wouldn't take *vous* from him, at least not the ones his age. Anyhow, in the mornings *tu* came easily to Dominique.

De Bizzi dropped the teaspoon he had been torturing for the past ten minutes. "I do have an answer," he said. "There aren't a million reasons a person could be so happy. You've heard from your mother again."

Everyone at 42-bis knew that Dominique's mother had raised him alone, when she had the time. All through his childhood and adolescence, Dominique had been put into foster care, then taken back by his mother, put in again and taken back.

"That's not it," he said. "That would have made me happy, sure. But I'm much more than happy, you've seen that."

De Bizzi twisted the teaspoon. "Give me a third chance?"

"Last chance, yes. You've got till tonight."

Friday, 12:20 P.M.

ROME,
Friday, 12:20 P.M.

"Hello," said Waldenhag, "Father Le Dangeolet? I'm glad I reached you; we're going to have to act quickly. Things are moving ahead. Nothing decisive yet, don't worry. Here's my situation. This business goes beyond me, and beyond my domain. I've decided to hand it over to people with greater authority than I. The pope should be informed. I just had Cardinal Chiaradia on the phone."

"At the Vatican? The secretary of state?"

"That's right. Well, he took me by surprise. I told him I had urgent business. He gave me an appointment in half an hour, at exactly a quarter to one. Tomorrow he'll be away from Rome; this afternoon he has a hundred things to take care of. It was either right now or much later on. Do you want to go with me? I arranged for two of us to come."

"Did you say who the second person would be?"

"I thought it proper to make you part of this move."

"Will I be able to state my viewpoint?"

"If I'd considered that inappropriate, I would not have invited you to come with me."

The *istituto*'s elderly porter had handed the provincial his telephone but stayed in his seat. He was all ears.

"Have you read the proof?" Le Dangeolet asked, as quietly as he could.

"I did read it, just at dawn. I don't have your concerns. I do have others. But this isn't the time to tell you them in detail. A car is picking us up in ten minutes at the Palazzo Pozzo. I'll wait for you there. We'll talk en route."

Friday, 12:25 P.M.

PARIS,
Friday, 12:25 P.M.

De Bizzi burst into the porter's office. "You're smiling, you're smiling, cut it out!" he said to Dominique. "I saw you through the door before I came in; you didn't hear me coming and you were smiling!"

"You didn't come here to tell me that," Dominique said mildly.

"Of course I didn't. Listen up. Here's my third answer. Your father's been found."

Dominique had never known his father. His mother called him "the bastard," or "the-bastard-good-riddance."

"That's not it," he answered. "I don't miss my father. Once in a while I come across some stranger and I say to myself, 'He's my father's age.' I look at him like a brother. The Father—our Father—is enough for me."

"All right, enough," said de Bizzi. He turned and left.

249

He hadn't guessed. Dominique mourned over that for a moment. A buzz at the switchboard straightened him up. In one sense he was relieved: de Bizzi might have questioned him about the right answer, and the few people who knew were bound to silence. "We've been asked to keep it to ourselves," Hervé Montgaroult had said. "Two or three days, no more—that's obvious."

Friday, 12:46 P.M.

ROME,
Friday, 12:46 P.M.

They had misunderstood the gesture—minimal, it's true—of the usher on the second floor. On the third they set off in the wrong direction. They saw their error at the dead end of a portrait gallery where the ancestors were all prelates. They reached Cardinal Chiaradia's antechamber at 12:46.

Le Dangeolet was no longer sure he held all that firmly to his viewpoint. Frankly speaking, he was no longer sure what his viewpoint was. And besides, viewpoint on what? He himself hadn't read the proof.

And the proof was indeed the proof, Waldenhag had just assured him. It displayed the divine reality, nature, presence. It was certainly of God. It would serve no purpose to seek further expert readings.

Like all great discoveries, this one owed its occurrence to a change in method. What did it matter whether Mauduit was the author or the instrument of that change—was there a distinction? From a resignation that he accepted—exhausted, heart-broken, and a mere step from despair—from that resignation came the slide to a last ember of hope. Hitherto separate fields of knowledge came into relation, by way of a simple idea within reach of the humblest person. Everything took on meaning. The interconnection was general, unquestionable, and so formally perfect it was awe-inspiring.

Waldenhag had spoken quietly in the backseat of the car. They had scarcely had five minutes, so he talked fast. Yet he did return to one point. The essential point, he had said.

Christians had a dualist idea of God that was terribly inadequate. The Most High, the Most Good—but God was in the Low as well, said Waldenhag. He was present at the very core of error, of failure, of the absurd; He was present at the core of evil.

Le Dangeolet had tried to engrave the lines into his memory. "With the world God created totality of being." "Everything that is has no other meaning but being." "Through the Creation, God explores in Himself the free play of being, of all being: good, evil, sense and nonsense, splendor and horror mixed." "What is, is nothing else but God in the process of being." "We are grounded in God, each person for what he is."

"Even the torturer?" grimaced Le Dangeolet.

"Even the torturer."

"God is indifferent to evil?"

"The Father accepts everything, since He is the

source of everything. But He suffers everything. There is no distance between the suffering of man and the suffering of God. And the Father risks everything in His creation. Because it is totality, creation carries within itself the germs of its own destruction. The Father is at stake there. The Son saves not only mankind, but in some way He also saves the Father. He justifies the Father's creation."

They were already entering Vatican City.

"You mentioned concerns different from mine," Le Dangeolet had said.

"Man informed of the proof will finally be free, his consciousness much elevated and his actions disinterested. On the other hand, knowing that God is in everything carries the risk of legitimizing any and all behavior. Remember what the five said yesterday: the brute may be confirmed in his brutality, the sadistic husband confirmed in his sadism, and so on. Amorality could take hold of mankind."

Le Dangeolet recalled his superior's expression of anguish. But what ought to have strengthened him, anchored him in his caution, instead undid any desire to intercede with the cardinal-secretary of state.

"I'm not sure I have anything much to say," he whispered to Father Waldenhag.

The latter did not answer. It was 12:47, and the double door at the far end of the antechamber was opening onto the impressive office of the Vatican secretary of state.

"Come in," said the cardinal, and Le Dangeolet no longer saw anything but him.

He had seen him before, but from afar, at the last general congress of the Casuists. Till now Le Dangeolet had been among those who joked about the man's grand manner. This time he had to restrain himself from gripping Waldenhag's hand.

Cardinal Chiaradia had the look of a prince. That's not often the case in princes, who frequently seem princely only when they are in full uniform. In Carlo Giuseppe Chiaradia, the look matched the rank, as rarely happens except in the theater.

The cardinal's rare height and slenderness were further accented by the black soutane. Snowy hair, smooth and close cropped. The features of a young star, seventy years old.

His adversaries claimed that the look had not been unhelpful in his career, and that even back in the seminary, professors seeing him pass by would say, "That one will go far."

Chiaradia had enemies. He was one of that species—actually quite sparse—of conservatives who are tremendously intelligent. His final arguments could rarely be countered, even though you knew you were right. So, offstage, you would mock the glorious physique.

"Come in," repeated the cardinal, coming forward to meet the two Casuists.

He placed a hand on the shoulder of each, welcomed them, and drew them toward a long table covered by a green rug. As he did so, he turned his head toward a window where a figure could be seen in silhouette. The Casuists recognized Archbishop Velter.

All four took seats at one end of the table, Casuists on one side, eminences on the other.

"Your Eminence," said Waldemar Waldenhag promptly, "here is the proof of God's existence."

He took the brown envelope from his coat and set it on the table.

"Have you read it?" asked the cardinal without seeming especially surprised.

"I have read it. Four of our best experts have read it. There is no doubt. As it happens, though, expert credentials barely matter here. What is stupefying about this document is that it compels recognition from anyone who sees it."

"So I have been told," confirmed Cardinal Chiaradia, nodding toward Archbishop Velter.

"You know about it?" the Casuists said together.

"We have been thinking of this exclusively ever since we were informed of it," said the cardinal forcefully. "Nothing else has mattered for us, and we were about to invite you to come discuss it with us when you called."

Velter said nothing. Waldenhag wondered if this "we" meant only the secretary of state in his royal entity, or the cardinal and the archbishop, or the cardinal and the archbishop and some third parties. Or else . . . or else the cardinal and the pope.

Chiaradia had laid his beautiful hand on the envelope, which he slid toward him.

"There are truths we do well to keep hidden," he resumed, his speech suddenly more rapid.

"What do you mean?" asked Waldenhag.

"The Church is not a trade union whose main goal is enlisting the most members possible. It is responsible for all mankind."

"You think the proof would do more harm than good for the world?"

"We ask you solemnly, both of you, to say nothing more and know nothing more about it. We charge you to secure absolute silence from those persons in the Society of Casuists and elsewhere who may have word of or knowledge of this text."

Waldenhag had gone pale, Le Dangeolet quite red.

"What does it mean, to stifle the proof of the existence of God?" uttered the general with enormous strain.

"It is not the first secret about God to be kept hidden in the Vatican," said the cardinal. "It will not be the last."

The envelope was gone from the table.

"Come along," concluded the secretary of state, rising and inviting his interlocutors to follow him. "Tomorrow you will be surprised to see how simply your life takes up its ordinary course again."

At the door he turned to Waldenhag. "Father Ortiz's latest book is troubling," he said. "We should discuss it."

Monday, 9:39 A.M.

PARIS,
Monday, May 31, 1999, 9:39 A.M.

The three knocks at his door made Le Dangeolet jump.

"Come in," he said in a voice he did not recognize.

It was only de Bizzi, come to do the press review, as he did every day at that hour.

"Do excuse my lateness," said the young man. "The newspapers are thick this morning."

He pulled his chair forward himself and sat down within reach of the provincial's desk.

"There's loads of coverage on Petitgrand, of course. The more murky an event is, the longer the glosses on it. I've made you a little collage. You'll see, it's rather comic. Petitgrand's single phrase to explain his resignation, citing 'the sudden irruption of meaning into my life'—that eight-word testament gives rise to the most diverse interpretations. They run from Machiavelli to Freud, going back and forth through dotty old Prime Minister

261

Deschanel wandering the railroad tracks in his pajamas . . . because finally the hypothesis most often put out is that the fellow's gone off his rocker—they say it a little differently."

Le Dangeolet didn't seem to be following. De Bizzi was not a man to be flustered by so little.

"The government will stay on until further word," he continued. "The president's office is holding consultations. They're talking about Torrin to succeed Petitgrand. Not so fast! howls the opposition, who want explanations, an inquiry. The whole thing is pretty funny."

Le Dangeolet wasn't laughing. De Bizzi moved on to the religious news.

"According to *Le Parisien,* they found the body of a priest in the Seine. That's not awfully serious—a priest who was more or less reduced to layman status, and who was a little odd besides—this fellow too. I wouldn't even be mentioning it if the archbishop hadn't sent a fax here to the province office a quarter of an hour ago, certifying that it was a suicide and asking for the greatest discretion on the matter. The poor devil was named Mauduit."

This time de Bizzi sensed he had caught his superior's attention.

"The Italian press has a puzzle as well," he continued. "Father Waldenhag is said to have disappeared. Do you know anything about that?"

"What's that chatter?" said Le Dangeolet slowly.

"He disappeared Friday, I read. People began to worry that night. What's disturbing is that the alarm apparently came from the Palazzo Pozzo. I'll stop with that now, you won't have any trouble finding out the real story. Just one quote, which shows the inventive genius of the Italian press: Father Waldenhag was supposedly spotted at dawn 'dressed as a garbage collector in Trastevere.' "

"Oh, please," said Le Dangeolet, his voice faint.

"More serious and more troublesome. *La Croix* announces that Fathers Michalet and Schmuckermann are quitting the Society."

"How about that," Le Dangeolet managed to mutter.

"Michalet is entering a Trappist monastery, Schmuck is apparently going off to be a hermit in the Swiss mountains. Neither one has given any explanation. The amazing thing is that you saw both of them here Wednesday morning!"

De Bizzi was pink with curiosity. Le Dangeolet collected his strength to put him off the scent. "Amazing, you're right. It's true they were feeling bitter about the Society. You know how theologians are. Nobody touchier. Can't bear the slightest reservation about their work. But never would I have thought last Wednesday that they were considering leaving us."

On his desk the provincial had the two letters from Montgaroult and Beaulieu. These two additional resignations were going to be hard to hide. Montgaroult was not well known, but Beaulieu, yes. And that their departures were coming at the same time would be much discussed everywhere.

De Bizzi, especially, must know nothing about it. He would have added things up right away: one Waldenhag plus one Michalet plus one Schmuckermann plus one Beaulieu plus one Montgaroult— total: five people Le Dangeolet had spoken with in the past week.

He should—what should he do? Deny the stories? And even if he did manage to stifle them, there could be chain reactions to worry about, unpredictable . . . what sort of thing? In what order? When you cap a spring, it's sure to burst through somewhere.

The provincial saw his secretary's eyes on him. "Nothing else?" he asked.

"No," said de Bizzi. "But, pardon me, you don't look well. . . . Is something wrong?"

"Everything is just fine," said Le Dangeolet in a whisper. Then, lowering his eyes to his desk, he saw that he was perspiring so heavily that drops of sweat running from his forehead were splashing stars on Beaulieu's letter.

Monday, 10:12 A.M.

Father de Bizzi was crossing the garden, his lips tight. Dominique felt sorry for him. He stepped out of the cubicle as de Bizzi passed under the portico. He was going to tell him everything. Too bad if he wasn't supposed to. He couldn't leave him in misery any longer.

"Jean, you want me to tell you the—" he began.

But de Bizzi wasn't listening.

"If anyone calls me," he flung back without slowing his stride, "you tell them I'll be here very late. I have a hellish schedule today."

Postface

"What is a pontifical secret?"

"A piece of information the Holy Father must not learn under any circumstances."

Vatican Chronicle, Summer 1995

About the Author

After studying political science and law, LAURENCE
COSSÉ was president of the European Community
Commission. She was a journalist for Radio France
and for the newspaper *Le Quotidien de Paris*. Her
current occupations include writing, working against
homelessness, and raising geese, ponies, children,
and freshwater fish. Cossé has written several nov-
els including *Les Chambres du Sud* and *Le Premier
Pas d'Amante*.

About the Translator

LINDA ASHER was a longtime editor at *The New
Yorker* magazine and has been a translator for over
thirty years. She translated Milan Kundera's last
several books from the original French; the most
recent is the novel *Identity*.